J.T. EDSON

THE BIG HUNT

HarperTorch
An Imprint of HarperCollins*Publishers*

HARPERTORCH
An Imprint of HarperCollins*Publishers*
10 East 53rd Street
New York, New York 10022-5299

Copyright © 1967 by Brown Watson, Ltd.
Copyright © 1968 by Transworld Publishers Ltd.
ISBN-13: 978-0-06-078430-0
ISBN-10: 0-06-078430-X

First HarperTorch paperback printing: March 2006

HarperCollins®, HarperTorch™, and ◆™ are trademarks of HarperCollins Publishers Inc.

Printed in the United States of America

Visit HarperTorch on the World Wide Web at www.harpercollins.com

10 9 8 7 6 5 4 3 2 1

Chapter 1

A MAN TIRED OF KILLING

~~~

It seemed that nothing could save the buffalo cow from death.

Concealed in a clump of bushes not two hundred yards away, Kerry Barran lined his sights on her rib cage at the right spot to make a lung shot. Under his right forefinger the set trigger of the Sharps Old Reliable rifle awaited the light pressure needed to move it rearward, release the sear and propel the striker on to the primer of a cigar-long .45/120/550 bullet in the breech. In his hands he held the ultimate in mid-1870's rifle power and accuracy. Driven by exploding five hundred and fifty grains of best imported British Curtis and Harvey black powder, the one hundred and fifty grains of lead—cast and patched by his own hands into the required shape—would rip into the cow's body, expanding and opening a large wound among the vital organs before coming to a halt against the hide opposite the point of entry.

With such a rifle, fired from a rest, a skilled man could not miss at short range. And Kerry Barran was skilled.

All his growing life he possessed the ability to hit a mark with a rifle. Even as a boy he carved his name as a deadly shot; not an easy thing to do when living among the accurate-shooting, rifle-wise men of Missouri. During the War between the States, he became a sharpshooter; the name given to special duty snipers assigned to pick off selected targets at long range. Since its end, he made his living with a rifle.

He might have lived out his life on the Missouri farm, doing no more than drop a buck, coon or turkey for the pot had it not been for the War; that terrible civil conflict of State against State which turned friends into bitter enemies and even set brother fighting brother.

At first the Barran family remained unaffected and unaligned. With the string of early victories to boost their morale, the Confederate supporters showed no concern or animosity over Pop Barran's neutrality. Not so the Yankees. Lane's Red Legs, a force every bit as ruthless, unscrupulous and unprincipled, as Dixie's Quantril, Anderson and Todd's bands, struck at Kerry's home. They killed his father and two brothers, strapped the boy to a tree and gave him a whipping from which he still carried marks.

That ended Kerry's neutrality. At sixteen he wore cadet gray and carried a rifle in a Missouri Infantry Regiment—a hard, foot-sore job for a young man used to doing most of his travelling on the back of a horse. He soon found himself in the thick of the fighting and his deadly rifle skill brought him notice from higher authority. General Longstreet took the young man into his personal command, and Kerry learned a different kind of war. No longer did he stand or lie in line with other men and pour random shots at a number of enemies. Instead, he worked with an experienced sharpshooter as his tutor, then alone, not to fire indiscriminately into the massed Federal ranks but selecting a definite target, aiming at it and driving home lead with deadly precision.

Kerry's mentor died, victim of one of the Federal Army's sharpshooters, and the young man fought a long-range duel against the Yankee's superior Sharps Berdan rifle. Emerging victorious, Kerry took the Yankee's weapon as his prize. It served him well until the meeting at the Appomattox Courthouse brought an end to military hostilities, if not peace.

Nothing remained of Kerry's old way of life. His home had gone, with Lane's Red Legs—now raised to the status of heroes—running Missouri, he turned West. The railroads pushed out across the start of the Great Plains and screamed for men to work on their construction gangs. Good pay and decent food being offered. Kerry took work as a gandy-dancer on one of the rail-laying crews. Having intelligence, a sense of command, the ability to handle men and a pair of hard fists to back up his play, he might have become a king-snipe, gang-pushing section boss with a future ahead of him in such work. Unfortunately, neither food nor pay came up to expectations. After a few meals of salt beef and weevil-infested biscuits, Kerry unpacked his Sharps Berdan and went out to shoot some fresh meat.

So able did he prove himself that he was taken from the construction crew and assigned to shoot camp-meat. At first that had not been too bad, for the hungry crews wasted none of the meat and even the hides found use. However, once they struck the great buffalo herds, things changed. With meat so easily obtained, the crews became fussy and wanted only the best cuts, leaving the rest to rot.

Kerry complained, but nobody listened. "Take a look, man," he would be told. "What we shoot out of the herds won't be missed."

And on the face of it, studying the mass of black, shaggy-humped bison, the theory appeared to be justified. Kerry could not accept it. Deciding he had come as far west as he wanted to, he quit the railroad and sought for a fresh start.

A homestead seemed to offer a decent way of making a living, and might have been, only a small herd of buffalo—not more than two or three thousand head—stamped the place flat in passing one day while he was visiting a near-by town.

Broke and hungry, Kerry accepted Cyrus Corben's offer to be a hunter, his work to shoot bison. Not until everything had been settled did Kerry discover that only the hides were needed. The rest, almost two thousand pounds of meat, was to be left where it fell, discarded as of no use. Back East, tanners discovered that the flints, dried buffalo hides, made good leather and paid well to obtain vast numbers. Corben needed to know only that. He did not care how much good meat went to waste as long as the flints came rolling in to Otley Creek, to be loaded on a train and shipped to the market in St. Louis.

Came to a point, smarting under the loss of his farm, Kerry did not greatly care either; at least not on his first couple of trips. Only this would make his fifth time out.

Living in such large herds, the individual buffalo possessed little instinct for self-preservation. So a man could, if he knew what to do, shoot as many of the great animals as he wished once he found a herd. Kerry could not help noticing that finding herds grew harder with each trip. Gradually the ceaseless inroads caused by hunting cut down what seemed numberless herds and where once a man could see the earth black with buffalo, he now found only small bunches—comparatively speaking—but mounds of bleaching bones.

A deadly efficient method of hunting had been developed by hide-hunters. Finding a herd the hunter stalked to around a hundred and fifty yards from the nearest animal and made his stand. Setting out his ammunition to be easily reached, he used a forked stick to support the barrel of his heavy rifle, then sat, or lay, whichever he preferred, and began to shoot.

First a cow, through the lungs so that she staggered, then stood with blood drifting from her nostrils. Scenting the blood, the bulls gathered and looked at the suffering beast, ignoring the occasional crack and sight of first one, then another of their companions sinking to the ground.

Fifty bulls a day Kerry reckoned to kill, the maximum number his skinning crew of four could handle. Often he took his entire quota from one stand. Even if the herd spooked and ran, the dull-witted beasts did not have sense enough to go far and soon halted. Then the hunter moved up, took a fresh stand and continued the slaughter. After which the skinners came, like turkey-buzzards swarming to a kill. Of all the grisly business, Kerry hated the skinning worse. Time did not permit for delicate work, nor would the sort of men who took on as buffalo hide-skinners be capable of it. Instead they ripped away the hides, using iron stakes to hold the carcass still, and dragging off the skin with horse-power.*

Kerry looked down at the unsuspecting herd before his stand. In his mind's eye he saw the cow stagger when the bullet struck, then stand and bleed away its life. It seemed he could already smell the blood, mingled with the acrid bite of burning powder. Then he imagined the brain-shot bulls, one after another, go down; sinking hind-first, then flopping to their sides, kicking spasmodically and going still in seconds.

Slowly Kerry's finger relaxed and the trigger moved back into its original position. Working the rifle's loading lever, he opened the breech and slid

---

* The system is described fully in the author's book TROUBLE TRAIL.

out the bullet. His eyes dropped to the wooden box at his side, built to hold six rows of ten bullets ready for easy removal and loading into the Sharps. One way and another, he did not expect to need the box's facilities again. Lifting the rifle from the Y-shaped rest, he let out his breath in a long sigh. Come what may, he had no intention of hunting for skins again. He placed the bullet in the box and closed down the lid with an almost symbolic gesture.

"Come on, Shaun," he said, rising to his feet.

Six foot one he stood in his calf-high Pawnee moccasins; with wide shoulders and trimming down at the hips. Cat-agile and light on his feet, despite his size, he gave the impression of latent, controlled and deadly power. Rusty brown hair, cut shorter than most buffalo hunters sported, showed from under his battered Jeff Davis campaign hat. His face had a rugged charm, yet stern, unsmiling gravity, tanned oak-brown by the elements and bristle-stubbed. Clean new buckskins, shirt and pants had not yet picked up the signs of his trade and smelled fresh. Around his waist swung a belt with flat-nosed Winchester .44 rimfire bullets in its loops and a razor-sharp steel fighting axe in Indian slings, but no revolver. All in all, he looked part of the Great Plains which gave him his new home.

Rising to his feet in a swift, fluid move more like that of a wild creature than a domesticated animal, Shaun, Kerry's Irish wolfhound, moved silently to his master's side.

No Irish wolfhound could be called small, and Shaun was big even for his breed. Full three foot high he stood, his hard-fleshed, steel-spring muscled body weighing over one hundred and fifty pounds; yet he moved with the ease of a much smaller dog. The dark brindle coat, hard and wiry to the touch, hid battle-scars and the left ear hung in tatters as mute testimony to the slashing sharpness of a cougar's claws—the mountain lion died soon after inflicting the wound.

Kerry came by the dog in the War and it had been his constant companion ever since. One day, ranging far ahead of his command, Kerry came upon a ruined Southern mansion. Its owner sprawled in death at the door, shot down as he fought to save his home. Standing over the body, gaunt with hunger and big even at so young an age, Shaun defied the sharpshooter to come closer. Not for an hour could Kerry approach the six month's old pup, and three more passed before he dare lay a hand on the lean, powerful jawed head.

Most likely Kerry would have taken the dog along only until he could find it a home, but for an incident that occurred soon after they left the looted house. Shaun, walking placidly alongside Kerry's horse—a sharpshooter rated a mount to carry him on his assignments—suddenly threw back his head and sniffed the gentle breeze. Many a dog would have barked on catching the distinctive scent of a man hiding with evil intent. Not Shaun. Low in his throat, rumbled a snarl and he shot forward like an arrow from a bow, launching himself among the bushes and tackling a Yankee soldier who crouched in ambush. However, the pup could not handle a full-grown man in its hunger-weakened state, so Kerry's rifle ended the affair.

After that nothing would induce Kerry to part with the dog. From that day, if Shaun went hungry, it meant Kerry had not eaten himself. Not that they often went hungry. Once fed up on good red meat, the dog grew in size, strength and stamina until it could keep pace with any horse. Soon Shaun could catch up, after a long chase, any but the swiftest whitetail deer and drag the animal to the ground unaided; or reach and hold at bay a full-grown bull elk until his master came with the Sharps and finished the cornered animal off.

Coming from Ireland's finest blood-lines—although Kerry never knew that—Shaun had the hunting instincts of centuries to fit him to his way of life. All the greyhound-type breeds, Scottish deerhound, saluki, borzoi, Irish wolfhound and the like tend to hunt by sight. Somewhere along his line, Shaun picked up a nose as keen as the redbone hound's and the inborn knowledge of how to use it. How well he used it showed by twice more steering Kerry from well-laid ambush; and on three occasions locating a hidden Yankee camp that might have passed unseen and unheard.

Even after the War, Kerry found reason to be glad to have the big dog at his side. A Negro in a checkerboard rock-roller crew* got drunk one night and swore to take the life of some stinking rebel peckerwood.† He made the mistake of selecting Kerry Barran as his victim. Razor in hand, the Negro crept into Kerry's tent—and left a damned sight faster than he entered. Shaun jumped the man even as he raised his hand to strike. By that time the dog had reached his full height, while eating regularly and well enough to fill out his huge frame. Before Kerry, the only man capable of controlling Shaun, could leave the tent, blood spurted from the Negro's severed jugular vein.

The incident, along with his growing distaste for the waste involved in meat-hunting to feed railroad gandy gangs, caused Kerry to change employment.

---

* Mixed white and Negro section gang engaged in clearance work.

† Negro's derogatory name for a white man from the Southern States.

He found himself working at something even more wasteful than shooting buffalo to take a few choice cuts of meat.

Turning away from the herd, he walked through the bushes to where, in a clearing some fifty yards from his deserted stand, he left his horse. The big iron gray gelding stood range-tied, with its reins dangling loose upon the ground but without its saddle. Should the buffalo chance to spook and run from before a stand, saddling up to follow gave them time to lose their fear and halt. Besides that, a horse left alone might take it into its head to lie down and roll; and would not allow the fact that it be saddled stop it. If around twelve hundred pounds of horse rolled on a saddle, it would not be the animal which came off second best.

Taking his saddle from where it lay concealed under a bush, Kerry walked over and caught hold of the gray's reins. He worked with easy precision, swinging the blanket into place and ensuring that it rode correctly, without wrinkles which might chafe the horse's back, and then dropping the range saddle on. A Winchester model '66 carbine sat in a boot on the left side of the saddle, its butt pointing up to the rear in a position for easy withdrawal. When skin-hunting in Indian country, a man needed something handier than the big, single-shot Sharps to defend himself against braves who, not unnaturally, objected to the wasteful destruction of their main source of food and clothing. The Winchester carbine served that purpose admirably, with its thirteen-round capacity, light weight and, at short range, man-stopping power.

With the gray saddled, Kerry mounted and rode back toward his camp, which had been set up some half a mile from where he located the herd on the previous night. Already the skinners had the four-horse team hitched up and lounged about the camp site for the shots which would tell them Kerry carried out his deadly work. Working with a man as skilled as Kerry Barran, the skinners knew that they would soon be at their task. Shooting fifty buffalo did not take long unless the herd spooked and even then there would be some bodies lying waiting to be skinned.

Although Kerry supplied work, food and pay for Potter, Wingett, Rixon and Schmidt, they came to him at Corben's recommendation and the hunter figured such loyalty that the quartet were capable of went to the storekeeper, not to him. Not that he minded. Crude, filthy in habits and thought, poor-spirited, the four men ideally suited their chosen field of life; but had none of the qualities Kerry regarded as necessary before accepting anybody as a friend. He let them get on with their work, ignoring them unless some specific task need be allocated. On their arrival at the stand to commence their grisly work, Kerry invariably rode away. Back in the camp he worked at reloading bullets and cleaning his rifle, and took no part in the lewd, foul-mouthed discussions of the quartet as they went about the business of preparing the flints for shipment.

Catching the sound of the gray's approaching hooves, Rixon looked around. He was a short, thin, scrawny rat of a man, vicious as a weasel in a hen house and truculent, hunting trouble when in liquor. Of all the quartet, Kerry cared least for Rixon. After a startled stare in Kerry's direction, Rixon swung around and spoke to the other skinners.

Judging by their reaction, none of the four liked the sight of the hunter returning. Potter, the big, hulking boss skinner, hitched up his blood-soaked pants and moved forward.

"What's up?" he asked. "Didn't hear you shooting."

"I'm through," Kerry answered. "Pack up and head back to Otley Creek."

"Through?" Schmidt, next in size to Potter, put in. "Why, you ain't even started yet this trip."

"Nor aim to," Kerry told him. "I'll see you back in town."

For a moment the quartet stood digesting the

news and not liking what it implied. In addition to the pay they received from Kerry, an extra sum came each man's way out of Cyrus Corben's pocket. Unlike Kerry, who paid the skinners by the day, Corben based his share on the number of skins brought in. None of the four considered their second employer to be a philanthropist—not that they knew the word—and were aware that no flints brought in meant no payment from the store-keeper.

"Cyrus Corben ain't going to like you going back empty-handed," warned Wingett, a lean bean-pole of a man with a face that many an undertaker might have wished to own for business purposes.

"I don't reckon he is," Kerry admitted, swinging from the saddle and drawing the carbine with his left hand as soon as his feet touched the ground. Not that he expected to need the weapon but because to have it in his hand had become as natural as donning his clothes in a morning.

"What about us?" Potter inquired sullenly.

"How's that?" Kerry asked.

"Where do we come off for pay?"

"I'll give you it for what you've done. Call it a week's work a man."

Which, as they were only a day out of Otley Creek and the men did nothing but hitch up and ride in the wagon, then make camp for the night, could be termed generous. Not that it struck the quartet in such a light.

"Corben ain't going to pay us happen you pull out!" yelped Rixon, his avarice causing him to forget that the storekeeper's payment should not be mentioned to the hunter.

"I never knew he did," commented Kerry, seeing the light on a number of things. "I hired you and fix to pay you for what you do for me. Anything you do for Corben's between you and him."

With that, Kerry walked toward where his bedroll lay packed ready to be loaded on the wagon should it become necessary to move camp. All Kerry owned in the world, less a small deposit in the Otley Creek Merchants' Bank, rested in the roll and he would never have left it at the camp except that he knew the quartet to be too afraid of his vengeance to touch it. Off to one side, picketed on good grazing, his sorrel mare snorted a welcome. She was a fine-looking animal, showing breeding, speed and stamina, and had won Kerry many a bet by her racing speed over a measured mile's rough range country going.

Cold anger creased Potter's face as he watched Kerry lay down the Sharps and reach toward the bedroll. Glancing at his companions, the skinner reached toward the knife at his hips. Shaun growled, deep and rumbling like the thunder in a distant storm. Powerful muscles bunched as the dog tensed, eyes full on Potter. Pivoting around, Kerry studied the hostile picture, for Potter froze immobile with his hand in the provocative position.

"I wouldn't try it," Kerry warned.

"Damn it to hell!" Potter burst out. "I was only going to loosen me knife."

"Last man who did that behind my back wound up with Shaun sat on his chest, eating his face," Kerry replied.

Not one of the quartet made another hostile move. Fear of the big dog held them in check, as did their knowledge of Kerry's dexterity in handling the carbine. While not a gunfighter in the accepted sense of the word, Kerry, armed with his carbine, could have walked away from a facedown with many of the fast-draw kind.

Collecting his property without any further interruptions or objections, Kerry saddled the mare and slid the Sharps into its long boot on her rig. Then he turned and mounted the gray.

"Mind one thing," he told the skinners. "That's Corben's wagon and team now."

In their vindictive rage the four men might have smashed or deserted the wagon, but not knowing that it belonged to the storekeeper. He would never forgive them for its loss and had the means to make them regret rousing his anger.

Until his master passed beyond revolver range, Shaun stood facing the men and watching their every move. Then a whistle sounded and the dog whirled, streaking away at a pace that would have made him a difficult target should any of the quartet try throwing lead after him. None attempted such folly, knowing that Kerry Barran's carbine could hit at ranges beyond their handguns' possibilities.

"What now?" asked Rixon.

"We go back," Potter answered. "Corben'll see he don't get away with it."

Chapter 2

A DAY FOR MAKING ENEMIES

THE SCREAM OF A DOG IN AGONY, MINGLED WITH a deep, savage snarling, ripped through the noontime calm of Otley Creek. Citizens of the growing railroad town who heard the noise did not need to ask as to its cause.

"It's Walt Sharpie's Bully dog at it again," one man said to his companion. "Some poor devil's dog's going under for sure."

Out in front of the Gandy Gang Saloon a big crossbred hound churned the street's dust as it stood over and savaged a collie pup foolish enough to cross its path. Standing on the saloon's porch, Walt Sharpie and a bunch of his regular cronies watched, laughing, yelling encouragement and making no attempt to stop the big dog, despite the pleas of a tearful boy tightly held in his mother's arms to prevent him trying to save his pup.

"Call it off, feller!" growled a cold, angry voice that did not belong to any child.

Sharpie swung his eyes unbelievingly in the direction of the speaker. Standing six foot in height, with heft, muscle and a deputy town marshal's badge to support him, Sharpie found few men willing to interfere with his pleasure. His eyes took in Kerry Barran as the hunter sat the gray, with the sorrel fiddle-footing nervously alongside it. Then the deputy's gaze went to where Shaun crouched by the horses, tense, watching the struggling dogs, but obedient to his master's command to stay put.

"Who the hell asked you to bill in?" growled Sharpie.

"I said stop your cur," Kerry answered.

"*You* stop him," Sharpie challenged.

"Shaun!"

Only one word left Kerry's lips. Like a flash the big wolfhound rose and charged forward. Sharpie roared out something and his dog looked up, seeing the approaching danger. Going at full speed, Shaun stretched right out and looked much smaller than his full size. So the other dog did not realize its danger. Big, heavy and hard it might be, but not compared with the huge wolfhound. Following its usual practice, Sharpie's dog hurled itself straight at Shaun. Such a tactic never failed to bowl the other dog over and leave it at Bully's flesh-ripping mercy until tried on the mighty bulk of Shaun.

Crashing full into each other, it was Bully who reeled under the impact. Shaun's momentum carried him forward and buckled the other's hind legs to tumble it over backward. Instantly Shaun struck. A mouth with jaws strengthened by tearing flesh and crunching gristle and bone opened, to close on Bully's unprotected throat, sinking home long, sharp, canine teeth with terrible crashing precision.

For once the gurgling screams of a dog in mortal agony did not herald another victim to Sharpie's savage Bully. Legs flailing wildly the dog tried to struggle out from beneath Shaun's crushing weight. Held under the jaw, Bully could not use his teeth in his defense and the relentless pressure on his throat gradually choked the life out of him; a process speeded by the wolfhound's canine teeth cutting through the neck's veins and arteries.

So sudden and unexpected had been Shaun's reaction to Kerry's command that none of the townsmen fully realized what was happening. Then it became apparent that for once Bully did not stand savaging a victim.

"Hey!" yelped Sharpie. "Get that cur offen Bully."

"*You* get him off," Kerry countered.

"By gawd, I will!" the deputy roared, and reached toward the Starr Army revolver at his right hip.

Tossing his right leg over the saddle, Kerry dropped to the ground. Even before he landed, his right hand collected the carbine from its boot. Lighting down with feet spread apart, legs slightly bent, he held the carbine hip-high and lined in the direction of the men before the Gandy Gang.

"Hold it!" he ordered, the lever blurring to feed a bullet into the breech.

Hearing the double click and noticing the practiced ease with which Kerry handled the Winchester saddle-gun, Sharpie stood still and forgot his intention of drawing and throwing lead into the wolfhound. At his back, Sharpie's companions assumed attitudes calculated to show their innocence and lack of objections.

"That's my dog being killed!" Sharpie gritted.

"And that's the boy's pup your dog was killing," pointed out Kerry.

"Shep's not the first dog that mean old Bully's killed!" yelled the youngster, pulling free from his mother's grip and running to where the collie lay whimpering as it tried to get away from the center of the street.

A convulsive thrashing of Bully's body almost dragged it free from Shaun's grasp, but proved to be no more than a final dying spasm. After the desperate jerking, the heavy cross-bred dog went limp and lay still.

"Come away, Shaun!" Kerry ordered.

Releasing his hold, the wolfhound moved clear of the bleeding shape and stood stiff-legged, hair bristling, the front of his chest matted with gore from Bully's torn throat. The youngster threw an admiring glance toward the big dog, but remained kneeling by his pup and cradling it in his arms.

"Good boy!" he enthused. "You sure taught that mean old Bully."

"Don't go near him, boy," Kerry warned, and repeated his order to the dog.

"What about my dog?" Sharpie demanded as Shaun returned to Kerry's side.

"Bury it," Kerry replied and, without taking his carbine out of line on the men, looked toward the boy. "How is he, son?"

"He—he's hurt, but I think he'll—he'll——" the youngster answered, face twisting in an effort to hold down tears of relief.

"You get somebody to help tote him along to

Doc Sherrin's office," said his mother and swung toward Sharpie. "Wait until my husband hears about this."

Just a touch of apprehension crossed Sharpie's face as he realized that he might have made a very wrong move in allowing his dog to pick upon that particular pet. Too late he recognized the woman as wife to a prominent surveyor of some importance on the Union Pacific Railroad; which itself carried a whole heap of weight around Otley Creek. One of his cronies, showing all the stand-fast loyalty of a rat on a sinking ship, left the side-walk and offered to help carry the injured collie to the veterinarian's office. With the rot once started, the remainder of Sharpie's companions moved away, dissociating themselves from his activities.

"Damn it!" Sharpie snarled, glaring at Kerry. "What about my dog?"

"I told you what to do," the big hunter replied.

Catching hold of the saddlehorn in his left hand, Kerry went astride the gray Indian-fashion, his feet not touching the stirrup irons until he sat erect. So swiftly had the move been made that Sharpie found no chance of taking advantage during the brief period Kerry could not have used the carbine. By the time he saw the offered opportunity, it had come and gone.

"I'll not forget this, skin-hunter!" Sharpie

warned, feeling that he ought to do something but unsure of what, when and how.

Kerry did not trouble to reply. Starting the horses moving, he continued his interrupted ride along the street. Breast wet with Bully's blood, Shaun moved after his master. Sharpie stood with a furious face but unable to think of anything adequate to say or do.

"And the Lord maybe knows why I did *that*," Kerry mused, "but I don't."

From the expression on that mean cuss of a deputy's face, Kerry reckoned he had made an enemy. Any smart-figuring man would be satisfied with the knowledge that his news was going to rile Cyrus Corben and avoid going around stirring up other troubles. Nothing Kerry had seen or heard about the storekeeper led him to expect a tolerant, understanding attitude when Corben heard of his decision.

Swinging to a halt before the long frontage of Corben's store, Kerry made use of the only free facility offered by its owner. So far Corben had not found a way to make money out of folks hitching their horses to his rail; but Kerry figured it was only a matter of time before he did.

Standing behind the center counter, raised slightly so as to allow him an uninterrupted view of the whole of his establishment, Cyrus Corben glanced at the door, looked down toward the cash desk and jerked up his head to stare again. His narrow slitted eyes in a shallow face took in every detail of Kerry's appearance and his rat-trap mouth grew even tighter. Rising on his tiptoes, Corben peered out of the glass-panelled top half of the door. The gray and the mare stood there, but no wagon.

"You had trouble, maybe?" he asked as the scout and dog halted before him.

"No. I've quit hunting."

Concern over the loss of a valuable wagon died from Corben's features and suspicion replaced it.

"How you mean, quitting?" he squawked.

"Just how I said. I'm through."

"You can't be through. There's buffalo out there yet if you look for them. You didn't go far enough out if——"

"I went out, found 'em and came back," Kerry answered. "I'm through hunting buffalo."

"And what about me?" Corben demanded.

"What about you?"

"I grubstaked you, fitted you out——"

"And've been paid back for it. You gave me the money, and I bought food, powder, lead, skinning knives—all off your shelves. Mister, you took it coming and going."

"You took my offer eager enough."

"And kept my part of the bargain. Your wagon's coming back with everything but one day's food still on it. I figure with what profit you make on it, we're about evens."

"You got no right to do this!" Corben wailed. "None at all. I've got your name on a grubstake contract——"

"Like I said, the wagon's coming back, still loaded."

"And what good does that do me? I could've sent out another man."

"And still can," Kerry pointed out.

"There's time been lost," Corben snarled.

"Two, three days, four at the most. What's that mean?"

"Two thousand dollars, that's what it means," squealed the storekeeper before he could stop himself.

"Two thousand, huh?" Kerry said quietly. "At fifty flints a day, I'd make at most eight hundred."

"So I made a bit of profit?" growled Corben.

"You made a hell of a good profit," Kerry commented, thinking back on the number of flints he brought in during his previous trips and estimating their value at the prices Corben inadvertently quoted: "Mister, the only thing I felt bad about was letting you down. Now it doesn't bother me any more, not one little bit. Get another stupid cuss to do your dirty work."

"I'll have the law on you!" shouted the store-keeper, leaning forward and slapping his palms on the counter's top. He jerked back even more hurriedly as Shaun reared up, placing big feet on the counter and giving out a low growl.

"Easy, boy," Kerry ordered.

The door of the store opened and a shadow fell in the pool of sunlight from it.

"You got trouble, Cyrus?" asked a voice.

Turning his head slightly, Kerry saw Town Marshal Berkmyer in the doorway. The marshal was tall, well built and sported the cutaway jacket, frilly-bosomed shirt, fancy vest and tight-legged trousers of a gambler. Around his waist swung a gunbelt, carrying a rosewood-handled Army Colt in a fast-draw holster. It had long been Kerry's theory that Berkmyer held his post by bluff. Sure the gunbelt hung just right, but Otley Creek lay a piece too far West for the owner to run into real gun-fighting men.

"There is no trouble," Kerry replied.

"There is some trouble," contradicted Corben. "I'm having a process served on you to take my money back."

"The wagon and supplies will cover that," Kerry drawled.

"I'm not having that!" Corben spat out. "That wagon's mine——"

"Not according to our contract."

"Then there's the supplies. I'll have the value of them off you, even if it means taking your horses and that fancy Sharps buffalo gun."

All in all, that ought to leave a margin of profit to satisfy even Corben. The gray gelding, of the deep-chested mountain-raised stock so favored by men who wished to travel far and fast, ought to bring in good money. Even more valuable, given the right market, would be the mare. Fast, agile, she could be sold as a racer, or for buffalo-running. Army officers on the Great Plains paid top prices for such a mount. Lastly, a Sharps Old Reliable rifle cost between a hundred and a hundred and fifty dollars new, but lost little in value while in hands as careful as Kerry Barran's. On top of that, the supplies in the wagon could be either sold in the store or used to feed another hunting party. Corben knew all of that—and so did Kerry.

"*You'll* take them?" asked the hunter.

"The law will!"

"If you get the judgment."

"I'll get it," promised Corben. "See if I don't."

"He sure enough will," Berkmyer put in.

Slowly Kerry swung around until he faced the marshal. His eyes ran slowly up and down the other's elegant shape, coldly weighing up Berkmyer's potential. Rumor had it that Corben exerted some influence and money to have Berkmyer taken on as town marshal and, if so, that meant he received a return for whatever he put out. Corben never spent a thin dime unless sure it would bring in at least a dollar profit.

"Just how do you figure in on this, then?" the big hunter asked.

"I'm marshal and responsible for keeping the peace."

"Can't see anybody breaking it. Or is pulling Corben's chestnuts out of the fire something else you get paid to do?"

"Can't say I like the sound of that," Berkmyer growled.

"Take your grief up with the judge, Corben," Kerry said, ignoring the marshal. "We'll have it brought out in court—happen you want *that*."

Something told Kerry that the storekeeper would not want too close an inquiry into the grub-stake arrangement. The local judge was a keen hunter and Kerry had taken him out on a couple of short trips after elk or bear. Not that that was likely to influence the judge, but he could be relied upon to rule fairly and not be swayed by Corben's position in the town. Come to a point, apart from the fact that a number of people owed him money—and repaid it at usurious rates—Corben had little standing in the town. Most folks would be only too pleased to see the storekeeper taught a lesson. In the final analysis, Corben would not want his dealing in the grubstake contract to be made public; not if he hoped to hire another hunter to replace Kerry.

Corben reached the same conclusions as the big hunter, and did not like them. Selling buffalo flints as a middle-man had proved one of the best investments he ever made, practically all profit and with very little risk. Such a deal possessed great charm to the avaricious storekeeper and he had no wish to see it slip away. Nor did he wish to lose Kerry's services. Good hunters were hard to come by, and were mostly working under other employment. A man like Kerry Barran, skilled in his business, conscientious, willing to work hard himself and push the skinning crews just as hard, could not be found on a street corner, or loafing in any saloon.

So the storekeeper wanted to retain Kerry's services and could see no way of doing so. Offering a better financial arrangements would not work. Money meant little to a man like Kerry Barran. Appealing to the hunter as an old friend might, only there had never been friendship between the two men. Corben knew enough about Kerry to see argument, or pleading, would have as little effect as the threat of taking him to court. Anger boiled inside the storekeeper, but remained in his control, for he was no fighting man.

"I'm not letting you get out of here like that!" shouted Corben, keeping a wary eye on the big dog, which now stood tense and watching at Kerry's side.

"Are you fixing to stop me?" asked Kerry quietly.

"This's Mr. Corben's property, skin-hunter," Berkmyer put in. "You keep a civil tongue in your head."

A smile twisted Kerry's lips, only it had no mirth and did nothing to soften the gravity and hardness of his face. Then he moved away from the counter, the wolfhound gliding along as silent and menacing as a stalking cougar.

"I'm going through that door, marshal," Kerry said flatly. "You're blocking my path."

There Berkmyer had it as plain as he could desire. Teeth drawn back in a threatening, challenging leer, fingers splayed out and hooked over the butt of his Colt, he stood full across the doorway. Silence dropped on the store, the three clerks and a couple of customers stopping their affairs to stare at the drama about to be enacted in the center of the room.

Otley Creek lay too far West for cowhands and other gun-handy men to be common, and for the most part the railroad workers preferred to settle their quarrels with fists, feet, pick-handles or such methods. So the situation before the people in the store held an element of high excitement. All knew their marshal claimed to be real good with his tied-down Colt, having, he said, been trained by such masters as the Earp brothers and other trail-end town lawmen. He had shown to good advantage on several occasions while doing his duty as keeper of the town's peace, handling trouble-causers with firmness and decision. Seeing his technique would make a conversation piece for weeks to come.

Behind the counter, Corben stood silent, trying to communicate mentally with Berkmyer and request leniency in dealing with Kerry. A hunter shot dead, or even crippled, was unlikely to bring in any profit, and profit ruled Corben's life. One thing the storekeeper knew, Kerry Barran did not intend to be prevented from leaving. How the affair went depended on what move Berkmyer made.

Watching Kerry advance, Berkmyer knew he faced a real challenge. Suddenly he realized that he did not face a drunken bohunk lumper,* or celebrating gandy dancer, against whom he scored his other successes, and neither of which type was noted for skill in the use of firearms. The man ad-

---

* Mid-European freight-yard laborer.

vancing so purposefully toward the door was Kerry Barran, ex-rebel sharp-shooter, buffalo-hunter and fully conversant with the rudiments and refinements of handling a gun.

At that moment Berkmyer recalled a couple of feats performed by Kerry with the carbine carried so negligently in his right hand. With two shots, the hunter tumbled a pair of turkey-vultures from the air as they glided down toward the rear of a railroad cook-shack. On another occasion, shooting from a distance of thirty yards, his first bullet severed the cord of a hanging bottle and the second shattered the bottle before it hit the ground.

Of course, uncanny accuracy like that did not necessarily mean a man possessed the mental state needed to cut loose and kill a fellow human being; but nothing in Kerry Barran's past life hinted that he would hesitate to kill should it become necessary.

Slowly, almost reluctantly, the marshal drew aside. He knew that word of his failure would pass around the town and hated the man who made him back water. However, he found that he lacked the courage to make a stand and face the consequences of his actions. Fury etched itself on Berkmyer's face as he watched Kerry walk from the room. For a moment the marshal thought of drawing his gun and shooting, but sanity prevailed. He could not throw lead fast enough to kill the hunter and save himself from the dog's attack.

Kerry stood for a moment outside the store, and the bitter, mirthless grin still played on his lips. First Sharpie, then Corben, and finally the marshal. It seemed to be his day for making enemies.

Chapter 3

A MIGHTY UNUSUAL FREIGHTER

"HEY, KERRY," CALLED A VOICE AS THE HUNTER walked back to his horses, ready to mount, " 'Tis back you are sooner than I expected."

Ma Gerhity came along the sidewalk, looking as plump, white-haired and motherly Irish as ever. Of all the people he knew, Ma came as close to being a friend as anybody. In addition to running a rooming house that was clean, comfortable and offered real good food, the old woman raised no objection to Kerry bringing Shaun into her home. While the wolfhound merely tolerated most folks, he accepted Ma and would even allow her to enter Kerry's room without giving any warning, touch his master's property—which meant anything that bore Kerry's scent—and even pat his head. Not that Ma often did so, being of the rugged, sensible kind who knew a dog should only be praised and patted when it did something to deserve it.

"I've quit skin-hunting," Kerry replied.

"Then your room'll be ready for you when you come."

"Well, Ma," drawled Kerry, glancing at the store. "The fact is——"

"Aren't you staying in town?"

"For a spell."

"Then you'll be staying with me like always," insisted the old woman. "What hotel would take you with that damned great darlin' beast along?"

"None, likely," Kerry admitted.

"Oh!" said Ma, noticing Kerry's glance at the store and realizing how his retirement might be received by Corben. "And is it trouble you're after having with that black-hearted skinflint?"

"A mite, Ma. I don't want to bring any of it on you."

"That you will not, the devil of a bit!" snorted the old woman. " 'Twill be a sorry day for me when the likes of Corben and his mealy-mouthed lawman cousin say who comes or goes at my house."

Knowing that to leave town at that time might

be construed as a sign of guilt, Kerry determined to stay on. He had been willing to live rough, sleeping down by the river and taking his food as it came, but preferred to stay in town. That way nobody could say that he hid to avoid meeting his obligations. Ma's house offered comfort and also a safe place to leave Shaun.

"If you reckon it'll be all right—" he began.

"That I do," Ma answered, throwing a glance at Shaun and seeing the dried blood on his coat. "Mercy me! What's happened to him?"

"Huh?"

"There's blood on him!"

"It's not his. He had a run-in with a dog belonging to a deputy."

"The saints be praised!" Ma exclaimed in delight, beaming at Shaun. " 'Tis long gone time that somebody settled the hash of that Sharpie's Bully. The brute's killed many a dog around the town."

"He won't kill any more," Kerry answered. "This's not my day for making friends, Ma."

While walking toward her house, the old woman tried to learn what kind of difficulty Kerry found himself in. Never one to expect help in sharing his troubles, the hunter told her only that Corben was considerably riled about his decision to quit hunting. Ma knew everyone in Otley Creek and could guess at the rest of Kerry's problems.

However, without showing far too much interest in his affairs, she could not offer to help. Nor did she know for sure just how she might give assistance. All in all, Ma felt pleased when her home came into sight, for it offered her a chance to change the subject.

"Looks like I've got more roomers," she remarked.

Kerry nodded, his eyes on the couple standing before the house and looking toward him.

Most Western trades wore a distinctive style or fashion of dress which identified the wearer to eyes that knew the range country. Buckskin jackets, levis pants tucked into low-heeled boots, long, coiled bull whips thrust into waist belts spelled freighter anywhere west of the Big Muddy. Not that Kerry felt surprised at the big, brawny man working at that trade. Handling a six-horse team took skill and a fair amount of strength, both of which the man looked to have in plenty. He dressed well and had an undefinable air about him which set him apart as a leader rather than one of the led.

The second of the pair, though; now there *was* a real surprise, nor did it grow less so the nearer Kerry walked and the more he observed. Standing five foot seven in height, that one did not look like the normal run of freighter. Few women did—and, mister, that for certain sure was a woman standing at the big freighter's side. Not even the fringed buckskin jacket could hide the fact. Her levis pants looked like they had been bought a size too small and shrunk during washing, and the shirt's front was unbuttoned low enough to dispel any lingering doubts as to her sex.

One idea for the girl's presence rose instantly to mind, then died again under closer scrutiny. Maybe the freighter liked his comforts and dressed the girl in such a manner to take her into Ma's respectable house. Only one would need to be blind not to see through that thin disguise. Besides, on going closer, Kerry found the girl far different from a brazen saloon-worker or denizen of a cat-house. Long hours spent in an unwholesome trade, with little time outside in the fresh air, left dissipated marks upon such women.

Only the girl showed no such signs. A U.S. cavalry kepi, perched jauntily on a mop of almost boyishly short red hair that framed a freckled, tanned, merry and refreshingly wholesome face. Not real out-and-out beautiful, maybe, but pretty enough and enhanced by a zest for life that glowed inside.

Ma clearly knew the couple and appeared to approve of the girl, despite the unconventional dress, bull whip thrust into the waist belt and ivory-handled Navy Colt riding butt forward in the fast-draw holster at the right side of those tight-stretched, well-filled levis pants.

Moving forward, the big man placed hands the size of hams on to Ma's shoulders, drew her to him and gave her a resounding kiss.

"You look younger than when I saw you last, Ma," he told her. "Dog my cats if I wouldn't marry you——"

"Only his wife won't let him," put in the girl, studying Kerry with interest, if not the predatory gaze of a woman wondering how much he might pay for her attentions.

"Now you went and spoiled it, Calam," said the man. "I'd have pulled it off this time if you'd kept quiet."

"That you wouldn't," snorted Ma. "I had the one worthless freight-hauling man in Rafferty, Lord bless his soul; and I've too much sense to take up with another." Following the girl's gaze, she smiled. "Kerry, do you know Dobe Killem and Calamity Jane?"

"Howdy," Kerry greeted, his dour face showing no expression.

Which did not imply that he failed to recognize the names. Dobe Killem was known as a top-grade freighter and owner of a good-sized outfit with a reputation for delivering its cargoes in the face of opposition.

From the first moment he realized that the girl was not Killem's added comfort, Kerry had a suspicion of her identity. Only the last trip he read a story about Calamity Jane in a fairly recent *New York Ledger* that found its way west and into his hands. The story claimed her to be a rich Boston girl, crossed in love and living on the Great Plains, performing man's work, so as to forget.

An interesting, entertaining story—but untrue.

Born Martha Jane Canary, the girl grew up wild and woodsy until her father died. Deciding that she could not bring up a family, Charlotte Canary left her children at a St. Louis convent and disappeared from their lives. Young Martha Jane had too much of her mother's wild spirit to accept convent discipline, and on her sixteenth birthday slipped off to hide aboard one of Dobe Killem's wagons. A full day's travel lay behind when her presence had been discovered. Even then she might have been returned in disgrace but for the indisposition of Killem's cook. Taking over his work, Calamity kept the drivers contented, and by the end of the trip had come to be regarded as a lucky mascot. From then on she worked with the Killem outfit. The drivers taught her how to care for, hitch up and handle a wagon team, to use a gun and wield the bull whip which served as tool, weapon and badge of office to their kind. Somewhere along the way, Martha Jane—the first part of which she cordially hated—became known as Calamity due to her habit of tangling in hair-yanking fights with jealous saloon girls and mostly managing to involve the rest of the outfit in a general melee while so engaged.

Despite the habit, Killem regarded Calamity as a valuable asset. She could drive a wagon with the best, take care of her load if the need arose, and possessed virtues many folks might never suspect. Being a woman never hampered Calamity in the performance of her work; and was a distinct advantage on the current chore.

Many a young man would have leapt at the chance of meeting Calamity Jane, but Kerry remained his usual, silent self. A sharpshooter led a lonely life; in fact, other members of his outfit tended to be wary of a soldier whose duty was to kill selected men rather than just tangle with and throw lead at the enemy in general. So Kerry made few friends. Nor had he found anybody among the gandy dancers who he regarded as worth befriending; the average railroad construction worker being semi- or completely illiterate, with no other interests in life than drinking, gambling, womanizing and discussing what bastards the ballet masters* were. Still less did he care to associate with the four men who acted as his skinners while buffalo hunting.

So Kerry, used to living a lonely life, became dour, shy almost, around strangers and silent in the presence of most people.

"Howdy," answered Killem, never one to force his company on any man.

"Say, what's that critter?" asked Calamity, indicating Shaun and grinning amiably at Kerry. "Danged if he's not big enough to be a wheeler in a wagon team."

"I tried it, but he sat down and wouldn't pull," answered Kerry and wondered why he spoke in such a manner.

"Likely he'd eat up the whole danged team at one meal," said Calamity, and turned to her employer. "Did you ever see so much dog in one piece in all your life, Dobe?"

"Can't say I ever have," admitted Killem.

"Come on in with you," ordered Ma. "And what brings you up this way, Dobe?"

"Some dude wants to go out hunting," the freighter replied. "Real big hunt, too. Going to last for near on three months."

---

* Section boss in charge of "gandy dancers."

"Reckon I'll go tend to my horses," Kerry remarked. "Have you room in the stable, Ma?"

"That I have," Ma affirmed.

Nodding to Calamity and Killem, Kerry led his horses off around the building in the direction of the stable. Shaun followed on his master's heels and Calamity watched them go. "You looked a mite surprised when he answered up to me, Ma," she said.

"Aye, I was that," agreed Ma. "Kerry Barran's a lonely man and don't take too easy to folks; but he's a real nice young feller."

"Can't say I'd want to be a skin-hunter," Killem commented.

"Nor does he, he quit this very day," Ma replied. "Not that I'm surprised. I've seen his face after he come back from a trip. He hated doing it. Say, where's your gear?"

"We left the wagons down at the livery barn and come around to see about rooms while we stay here."

"And how long'll that be?"

"Two, three days, it all depends on whether our dude arrives on the westbound train today and if he's ready to pull out again after the trip."

"Them Eastern dudes tire easy after a trip on one of our trains," Ma said. "Where's he from, New York?"

"England," Killem replied. "He's a lord, or some such, so the Lord knows what he'll expect."

"Got his wife along," Calamity put in.

"That's why I brought Calam with me instead of one of the boys," Killem went on. "Figured her and the dude's missus'd be company for each other."

"As long as she don't get all hoity-toity with me——" began Calamity.

"You mind what I told you, Calam gal!" Killem growled. "Ma, so help me, if this red-headed lump of perversity——"

"Isn't that the train whistling?" interrupted Calamity, cheerfully ignoring her boss's threats.

"Sounds like it," agreed Killem.

"He's early today," Ma commented.

"Sounds that way," Killem answered. "Come on, Calam, let's go see what our passengers look like."

On arrival at the railroad depot, Calamity and Killem stood at the rear of the usual crowd gathered to witness the day's premier attraction. Bell clanging, steam hissing, the train drew to a halt. People descended from the cars, some to be greeted by relations or friends, others strolling off with the air of knowing their way around Otley Creek, and a few who stood looking about them in the interested but lost way of strangers.

"No sign of them," remarked Calamity, for none of the strangers had the appearance of being wealthy enough to make the long journey from England merely to enjoy a holiday. "Maybe——"

At that moment a tall man emerged from the front car, swinging to the ground with agile ease and turning to help down a woman. Calamity did not end her words for she guessed the couple must be her boss's clients. Certainly the man did not hail from the range country, or if he did had bought his clothes elsewhere and not west of the Mississippi River. A tan-colored felt derby hat, with a dented crown and deeply rolled brim, sat rakishly on his tawny hair, an unusual form of head-dress to be seen on the Great Plains. Cut low hip length, the tweed jacket's back gathered in slightly to a belt buttoned at either side. His trousers, also tweed gathered in at the knee, being tucked into long gaiters, and shining boots finished his outfit. Literally finished it, for he did not appear to be wearing a gun.

The woman stood about Calamity's height, with blonde hair showing from under her small, neat, practical hat. Beautiful features, calm, showing intelligence and breeding, studied the town with interest, but showed no hint of distaste. A travelling suit of dark blue, which did not show the signs of use as would most colors, set off a rich, mature figure and a cloak of golden seal's skin hung open over her shoulders. All in all, Calamity concluded, looking the blonde over, there stood a tolerable heap of woman.

For a moment the man and woman stood by the train and looked around them. Keen blue eyes in a tanned, strongly masculine face rested momentarily on Calamity and studied her with approval, then swung toward Killem. In that moment Calamity gained the impression that there stood a man who, no matter how he dressed, it would not pay to rile. A neatly trimmed moustache and short goatee did nothing to hide a firm mouth with grin quirks at its corners.

"You'll be Mr. Killem," said the man, walking forward with the stride and swing of a soldier used to commanding obedience yet not arrogant with it.

"That's me," admitted Killem.

"I'm Lord Henry Farnes-Grable," the tall dude stated, his voice a clipped accent Calamity had never heard before and far different from the dialects of such Englishmen as she had met. "Don't look surprised, old chap, General Sheridan described you rather well."

"Yeah," grinned Killem, and held out his hand. "I just bet he did."

A hand strong and hard took Killem's and shook it. Whatever he might be, that drawling

Englishman was no milk-sop who needed wet-nursing.

"Beryl, this is Mr. Killem," introduced Lord Henry, turning to the blonde. "Mr. Killem, my sister."

Smiling, the blonde held out her hand which Killem gingerly took after giving his palm a rub against the leg of his pants. Not exactly an ignorant rustic, Killem still felt like a barefoot country boy when looking at the poised, calm face of Lady Beryl Farnes-Grable. Then he lost his embarrassment, for she possessed the rare virtue of being able to set people at their ease.

"I'm quite looking forward to the trip, Mr. Killem," she said.

"Hope we give you a good time, ma'am," Killem answered. "This's my driver, Martha Jane Canary."

"My pleasure, Miss Canary," said Lord Henry and took the girl's offered hand.

"We've got a long ways to go, and I've never been one for being called 'Miss,'" Calamity answered. "Why not make it 'Calam,' like everybody else?"

"It's short for Calamity," Killem told the Englishman. "And she's all of that. But there's not a better driver on the Great Plains."

"Of course," Lord Henry replied. "You're

Calamity Jane. General Sheridan told me about you."

"I was hoping to meet you, Calam," Beryl put in, offering her hand.

Calamity based her ideas of a person on the way the other shook hands. Film, strong—surprisingly strong after preconceived ideas of the pampered life a lady led—Beryl's grip satisfied Calamity that the blonde would do as a friend. For her part, Beryl studied Calamity and liked what she saw. There was something refreshingly different about the red-headed Western girl; and it went beyond her unusual style of dress. At twenty-eight, Beryl no longer regarded defiance of convention as an automatic sign of worthiness. However, she felt that Calamity Jane would make a good friend, or just as bad an enemy. Born into the English aristocracy, Beryl was no snob—her kind rarely were, that being the way of the newly-rich who felt unsure of their position—and knew she would be thrown into very close contact with Calamity throughout the trip. Things would be much more pleasant if a friendly relationship could be maintained.

"Where's Frank Mayer?" Killem asked, looking around for some sign of the hunter who arranged for his wagons to come to Otley Creek.

"We ran into a bit of difficulty there," Lord Henry admitted. "Mayer broke a leg running buffalo, whatever that might be, the day before we were supposed to meet. However, he said that your scout could take his place."

"He could," agreed Killem. "Only I didn't think to need him with Frank on hand and left him with my main outfit."

"Can we manage without a hunter?" asked Beryl.

"I wouldn't want to try, ma'am," Killem replied. "Sure I've done some hunting in my time, but I'll have work to do around the wagons. Have you any staff along?"

"Wheatley, my valet, is all," Lord Henry answered, nodding to where a tall, lean man wearing sober black of the cut and style adopted by the poorer classes stood by the baggage car and watched the Negro porters lift out a large trunk. "Didn't want a big staff along."

"So, of course, I had to do without my maid," smiled Beryl.

"That's men all over," grinned Calamity. "Never seen such mean critters. Say, is that all your gear?"

Three trunks, a long leather case with reinforced sides and two smaller boxes that looked like the kind used for shipping bulk orders of ammunition, stood by the train, watched over by the tall man, his attitude showing that he expected no more to come.

"Yes," Beryl replied. "We always buy our supplies on the spot, it saves time and space."

"I'll see to getting it down to the Bella Union Hotel," Calamity promised. "Got their best rooms—Hey, we only asked for one room, thought you were married."

"If you wish, Henry," Beryl said, "I will go with Calam and book another room."

"Go to it, old thing," he answered. "Now, Mr. Killem——"

"Make it 'Dobe,'" the freighter suggested, throwing a warning glance at Calamity, for she alone of his outfit knew his name to be Cecil.

"Now, Dobe. About the hunter. Could we get anybody?

"There's young Bill Cody, but he's working for the railroad, or the Army," Killem replied. "Or maybe——"

"How about Kerry Barran?" Calamity put in. "Now he's quit skin-hunting, he might take on."

"Could be," Killem admitted guardedly.

"Is there something wrong with him?" asked Lord Henry, noticing the big freighter's hesitation.

"Not as I know of. Only he's a strange one, don't make friends easy——"

"He's just quiet," Calamity objected.

"Likely," grunted Killem.

"If you think he would do," Lord Henry said, "I see no objection to asking him to act as our guide. Think about it, Dobe, while we're going to the hotel."

Chapter 4

A NIGHT FOR MAKING DECISIONS

THE CHANCE TO SOUND OUT KERRY BARRAN DID not present itself until evening. After settling his belongings into the usual room at Ma Gerhity's place, Kerry took his horses and dog along to the nearby river. Allowing Shaun to swim, so as to wash the matted blood from his coat, Kerry settled down on the river's bank and gave thought to his future.

While the Army needed scouts, the idea did not appeal to Kerry. During his time as a meat hunter for the railroad, he saw enough of Indians and scouts to know he could handle the work; but memories of the War prevented him from considering working alongside blue-clad Federal troops.

California struck many people as the pot of gold at the end of the rainbow, but not Kerry. The days when a man might dig up a fortune had long passed and all the gold-producing areas lay in the hands of the big companies. Farming in California might be attractive, yet Kerry knew that starting up required capital and knowledge. All he learned as a boy on a Missouri farm had long since been forgotten and most likely would not apply to conditions in the Bear State.

Of course he might head South, down into Texas, and take work on a ranch. While he had no experience of cattle work, he figured he could learn. It meant starting from the bottom, unless he went in for breaking horses. The thought had possibilities. Kerry possessed a way with horses, including the uncanny but very necessary knack of knowing which way a bad one intended to go when it bucked. In a land where a horse was a way of life, instead of a mere means of transport, a man who could tame bad ones could always find work.

The more Kerry thought of the idea, the better he liked it. Busting horses brought in good money and left a man his own boss. If he took care, he might be able to save enough to buy a small place and raise his own horses for sale.

Time passed as he relaxed by the river and suddenly he became aware that the sun hung low over the western horizon. Most likely Ma would be worrying herself into a muck-sweat over his absence. He had best get back before she took out after Corben with a broom handle, blaming the storekeeper for his failure to return. Knowing Ma's temper when riled, Kerry did not doubt that she would do so.

With Shaun at his side, Kerry collected the horses and rode back into town. He went along at the rear of the main street and saw a wagon he recognized standing behind Corben's store. From the look of the lathered team horses, the skinners had pushed them hard. That figured for the men to be in town already. Nor did the lack of interest in the horses' welfare surprise Kerry; he had been forced to take a firm hand with the quartet over such neglect before. Ignoring Rixon, who glared at him from the rear door of the building, Kerry continued to ride on in the direction of Ma's place.

"Barran just rode by," Rixon told the men in the rear room of the store.

"What're you aiming to do with him, boss?" asked Potter, looking at Corben.

The storekeeper did not reply for several seconds. Although Potter hinted on his arrival that he could take over the hunter's work, the idea had no attraction in Corben's eyes. Nothing about Potter convinced that storekeeper of his ability to handle the hunter's responsible job.

"I'm going to make him come crawling back after work," he finally said.

"How?"

"Get him in trouble with the law."

"You mean, blame him for a robbery?" inquired Rixon.

"No!" Corben snorted. "That way he'd go to jail and be no use to me. I aim to have him fined so heavily that he'll have to come work for me, or lose everything he owns."

"How're you going to do it?" Potter wanted to know.

"He's going to pick a fight with you four."

"*Us?*" yelped Wingett.

"You four," agreed the storekeeper. "Give him a beating he'll never forget."

"Yeah, but——" Potter began, seeing several objections to the scheme.

"I'll pay any fine you might get—not that you're likely to have one slapped on you. There'll be Deputy Sharpie on hand, ready to act as witness that Barran caused the trouble. And Marshal Berkmyer always listens to his men."

"Should be all right then," Potter stated. "I've wanted to take the tar out of that damned hunter for a spell now."

"You'll have your chance tonight," Corben promised. "Look around town for him. The more damage you can do, the better, so don't jump him in the street."

"Why not get him in the store?" asked Wingett.

"Oh sure!" scoffed Corben. "And have my stuff damaged. You get him in the Gandy Gang, or the hotel, whichever he goes to, and do it there."

While wanting Kerry Barran back, Corben did not intend to risk damage to his property or hide. Already that day he had paid out a good sum of money for a herd of cattle brought in after purchase at a trail-end town along the track and felt he made a sufficient expenditure for one day; even though the beef would bring in a good profit. So he wanted the hunter handled as cheaply as possible. Potter's bunch came real cheap—and Corben hoped that none of them realized they could hardly be kept in the same hunting party as Barran after they worked him over.

"You sure that deputy'll be on hand?" Potter said.

"He will," assured Corben. "And he doesn't like Barran since that damned great cur killed his dog this morning."

Knowing that Kerry never took Shaun with him around town, the four men felt no concern over the mention of the wolfhound. All wanted revenge on the man who they considered deserted them; and also for the times when he forced them to do work against their will. Potter looked at the others and caught their nods of agreement.

"All right," he said. "We'll do it for you."

"Go now, I'll have my clerks tend to your team and unloading the wagon."

With such an inducement, the quartet needed no further urging and left before any of them could think over the possible consequences of the proposed attack on the big hunter.

In addition to its other facilities, the Bella Union Hotel in Otley Creek operated a good-sized bar with all the usual saloon amenities. A chuck-a-luck table's cage whirred and the dice chattered as a few gandy dancers stood around and tried to beat the house's 7.47/54 percent advantage. Other members of the section crew indulged in different pleasures, varying with their interest in either enjoying female society or trying to win money. At the bar a couple of boss-snipe watched their men indulgently while entertaining two of the room's half-dozen girls.

Dobe Killem and Lord Henry entered the bar-room, followed by the lean, angular valet, Wheatley. Only the two girls with the section bosses at the bar gave the new arrivals any attention. One of the pair, a buxom brunette called Big Win, nudged the other and nodded toward the Englishman.

"He looks like a sport who'd like company, Kathy," she said.

"And what about us?" asked one of the king snipe.

"The boss likes us to circulate," Kathy answered. "But we'll stop and finish our drinks."

"That's him, standing alone there at the end of the bar," Killem remarked, leading the way across the room toward where Kerry Barran leaned on the counter and toyed with a drink.

"Order drinks for us, Wheatley," Lord Henry told his valet. "Try their Old Stump-Blaster, I've heard it recommended."

"Yes, sir," Wheatley answered, and caught the bartender's eye.

"Are you doing anything special, Kerry?" Killem inquired. "I mean, now you've quit hunting."

"Nope."

"Would you be interested in going out on a three-months' trip?"

"Doing what?"

"Let's find seats, shall we?" Lord Henry interrupted. "My old father used to tell me it's folly to stand when you can sit, and madness to sit when one can lie down."

"How about it, Kerry?" asked Killem.

"Sure," the hunter answered. "There's a table empty."

After watching the three men take seats at a table, Big Win finished her drink and left the two king snipes to walk forward.

"Hallo," she greeted, right hand on her hip and her most winning smile directed at Lord Henry.

"Good-bye," Killem replied. "We're talking business."

Annoyance glowed in Big Win's eyes, but she knew better than make a fuss when dealing with such an important-looking customer. Turning, she walked back to where her friend stood with the section bosses. Nor did the grins of the two men do anything to lessen her anger.

"That damned freighter!" she spat out. "I'd like to fix his wagon."

"Maybe you'll get your chance," said one of the king snipe. "Come on, Bill, let's go see what they're doing at the Gandy Gang."

Watching the departure of two men who might have spent more money, Big Win did not lay any blame on her own actions but directed it at Dobe Killem's innocent head. She swung her angry eyes to watch Wheatley carry a tray with a whisky bottle and glasses to Killem's table and then turned her attention to finding some other source of drinks. Deputy Marshal Sharpie entered the room and made his way to the bar, but she knew he was of no use. So she stayed by her friend and wondered what business the dude might have with Kerry Barran.

"I would like to hire you as a guide, Mr. Barran," Lord Henry said, waving Wheatley into a seat after the man poured out drinks. "Take one yourself, Wheatley."

"Doing what?" Kerry asked.

"Hunting."

"You mean for sport?"

"Of course," the Englishman answered.

"Sorry," said Kerry. "I've done hunting."

"They do say that once a man is bitten with the hunting bug, he'll never give it up," Lord Henry commented.

"I have," Kerry assured him. "Thanks for the drink."

"You won't change your mind, Kerry?" Killem put in.

"Nope."

"So be it," Lord Henry said. "We'll just have to try to get somebody else."

"It'll not be easy," Killem warned. "Apart from Kerry here, all the good men are already hired."

"Then we'll go without a guide," Lord Henry stated. "Perhaps I can trade on your good nature, Mr. Barran, and ask for advice."

"Go ahead," Kerry answered.

"Any details you could give me about the game will help."

"What're you after?"

"Elk, bighorn sheep, antelope, maybe a whitetail buck, grizzly bear of course, cougar, anything else that comes along."

"You can get an elk not more than a mile from town, with luck," Kerry said.

"I daresay I could," Lord Henry replied. "Saw some coming in on the train. Nothing really exceptional though. Where would you say the animals with the best heads are found?"

"Up in the high country. Old bucks in their last year with a herd, or just been run off by a younger critter."

"Which sort don't often come near to a town, they know better," commented the Englishman. "That's what I'm after. An old buck with a really fine spread of antlers, and whose use to the species is about over."

Looking at the lean fighting man's face, Kerry read interest and eagerness on it. There sat a man who loved hunting so much that he did not care for an easy trophy but wanted to take the best specimen available and was willing to work hard to do so. On hearing that the Englishman planned to go hunting, Kerry pictured a luxury filled, leisurely trip across the Great Plains, shooting at everything that came in sight merely to see how many animals could be killed. He noticed that Lord Henry did not mention buffalo and put the omission down to avoiding the obvious. Every dude who comes west wanted to tumble buffalo, either from a stand or by running a herd from the back of a horse.

"Where'd we make a start at finding big ones, Kerry?" Killem asked.

"Up the Wind River way's as good a starting place as any. You'll be headed into country where you can pick up most of the others, too. I saw some real big old whitetail bucks up there, bighorns too in the real high stuff. Where you get them you'll find grizzly and cougar."

"Do you know it, Dobe?" inquired Lord Henry.

"Nope, but likely my Army maps'll show us where to go."

"And the antelope," the Englishman continued, turning back to Kerry. "How about them?"

"They run pretty much to one size. Trouble with them's not picking the biggest, but getting close enough to shoot."

"Alert, are they?" Lord Henry inquired eagerly.

"Real alert," agreed Kerry. "And live in open country. You can try to run them down on a horse, but they'll get away most times; or wait for them to come down to a waterhole."

"Is there no other way?"

"Stalking them on foot, but it's not easy."

"If it was, I wouldn't want it. That's what I'll try. How about cougar, can one bait them up?"

"How's that?" asked the hunter.

"Stake out a kid or calf and let its bawling attract the cougar's attention. Then when the cougar comes in, you're waiting hidden close by and drop it. That's one way I used to shoot panther in India."

"Does it work?"

"That depends on the panther—and how well one makes one's hide. Of course, with a man-eater, one tries to have it go for the bait, not oneself."

For the first time in his life Kerry began to realize what a hold hunting had on him. Suddenly he wanted to talk; and to listen to this tanned dude who appeared to know a fair bit about hunting.

"I've never heard of anybody trying that with a cougar," Kerry admitted.

"How about sitting up over a kill and waiting for the cougar to return?" suggested Lord Henry. "That's another way we go for tiger and panther in India."

"That's another one I've never heard of," Kerry replied. "Way to get a cougar, run him down with a pack of hounds."

"Isn't that a shade too easy?"

"Depends. I've seen a cougar run for eight, ten miles ahead of a pack afore it treed. And up the Wind River country you'll not be able to ride a hoss much. So it means running the hounds on foot, trying to keep them in hearing distance."

"Now that sounds interesting," Lord Henry said, eyes alive with interest. "I've hunted with the best packs in England and always seen good sport. But that was after fox, not cougar."

"One'll run before hounds, just like a fox," Kerry answered. "And give the hounds a fight happen they catch it where it can't tree."

"Where would one get the hounds?"

"There's an old-timer here in Otley Creek has three of the best cat-hounds I've ever seen," Kerry replied. "Unless that damned fool I had a run in with this morning's dog jumped them."

Remembering the incident, Kerry became sure that the man he mentioned stood at the bar. Glancing across, Kerry found Sharpie's eyes on him, glowering viciously. Finding himself observed, Sharpie looked away and saw the four skinners had just entered the barroom.

Kerry also saw the new arrivals, but thought nothing of their presence. The Bella Union made no attempt to keep customers out, although it kept a section available where the visiting silk hats might entertain away from the revelling *hoi polloi*, so Kerry suspected nothing. None of the four gave him as much as a glance as they crossed the room toward the bar.

"Say, we're empty," Kerry said. "I'll go get another round."

Before any of the others could object, the hunter rose and walked from the table. Killem and Lord Henry watched him go and then exchanged glances.

"You've got him interested," Killem stated hopefully.

"I hope so, he could make this trip a success— no offense, Dobe."

"None took. I know what you mean. Sure I've done some hunting, but my work's freighting, and I don't claim to know hunting like he does."

"Hey, boys," Potter said in a carrying tone as Kerry approached the bar. "Just take a look at who's here."

"It's that high-toned skin-hunter, Mr. Kerry Barran," Rixon went on, showing signs of having taken enough drink to become truculent. "He's a big man now, though, doesn't want to go skin-hunting any more."

Of all the quartet, Kerry disliked Rixon the most. Filled with an embittered spirit at knowing himself to be a failure, hating everybody who showed any sign of success, Rixon was cruel, vicious and untrustworthy. Sober, he practiced minor cruelties that revolted Kerry; drunk, he became fighting-wild and dangerous when backed by the other three.

Wishing to avoid trouble, Kerry swung away from the quartet. Rixon weaved across, keeping before the big hunter, his face twisted in lines of hate.

"Big man, that's Kerry Barran," the skinner went on. "Real important. All he does is ride out and shoot buffaloes in the morning, then leaves the dirty work to us. Only he's made so much money at our expense that he don't aim to work any more."

Suddenly the hunter sensed danger, feeling it as a deer knows when a bear is hungry and must be avoided. He recollected that none of the trio looked in his direction on their arrival. If it came to a point, they took pains to avoid turning their eyes in his direction. Along the bar he noticed that Deputy Marshal Sharpie stood with his back to the skinners, staring with fixed intensity at a vingt-un game in progress across the room.

The last thing Kerry wanted at that time was trouble. All day he had thought hard about his future and swore to reach a decision that evening. Until his arrival at the Bella Union bar, he had been almost decided to try his hand as a horse-breaker.

However, the Englishman's offer sounded mighty tempting, even to a man grown tired by the wanton slaughter of hide hunting. So the last thing Kerry wanted was to become involved in a brawl.

Again he tried to avoid the man, moving the opposite direction, but Rixon followed him, still blocking his path.

"Get out of my way, Rixon," Kerry said quietly.

"Listen to that, boys," Rixon yelled. "He's still giving us orders. He reckons he's the big boss man, even after he quit and run out on——"

Laying the palm of his hand on Rixon's face, Kerry shoved hard and the man shot backward to crash into the bar.

"Tough against a little feller, ain't he?" demanded Potter in a mock sympathetic voice.

Kerry realized that he had been edged around so that Potter and Wingett stood just before him. Only two of them. No sign of the hulking Schmidt. He read the threat on the two men's faces as they started to move in his direction. Alert for danger, Kerry caught a flicker of movement from the corner of his eye. Arms outstretched to enfold the hunter in their grasp, Schmidt lunged forward from where he had moved while Kerry watched Rixon and the other two.

Chapter 5

A LADY FORGETS HER REFINEMENT

~~~

WHILE WELL PLANNED, CONSIDERING THE SOURCE from which it sprang, the attack failed to achieve full success due to Kerry's lightning-fast reactions and the knowledge of *savate* he picked up during the War. Not the graceful, stylish *savate* practiced by the rich French-Creole bloods of New Orleans, but the raw, basic, pure-fighting variety of the Cajun swamp-dwellers of the South.

Swiftly Kerry kicked sideways, balancing himself on the right leg while the left aimed at a point on Schmidt's body calculated to make him lose his aggressive tendencies if caught. Unfortunately, in his haste Kerry aimed just a mite high. His foot, rock-hard under the moccasin, caught Schmidt in the belly and stopped the German's rush. Giving a grunt, Schmidt reeled back a couple of paces, his face showing the pain he felt.

Coming into the attack, Potter saw Schmidt's part of the plan fail and threw a long looping blow at Kerry's head to catch the hunter on one leg. Kerry went into the bar, hitting it hard. Out whipped Wingett's fist, smashing into the side of Kerry's head. Pain and dizziness whirled through Kerry and he fought to keep on his feet. Once down, he knew he would be completely at the quartet's mercy—and they would show him none. Rixon sprang forward, kicking viciously to drive his boot toe into the side of Kerry's shin and sent further pain through him. Once more Potter hit, then Wingett ripped another blow into Kerry, further preventing him from recovering. Given a few seconds' respite, Kerry could have fought back, but the sustained attack prevented him from gaining it.

At his table, Lord Henry watched the opening moves of the attack. The moment it became obvious that a multiple attack was being launched, the Englishman sent his chair over and came to his feet. Clearly Wheatley knew what to expect, for he also rose and took the jacket which Lord Henry peeled off and accepted the watch that the other removed from his vest pocket. With that done,

Lord Henry crossed the room in the direction of the bar. So quickly had the Englishman moved that Dobe Killem just sat and watched.

"Fair play, you blighters!" Lord Henry balked. "Give him a chance."

Hearing the voice, Wingett glanced around and saw the tall Englishman approaching. Noting the white shirt, stylish vest, immaculate collar and sharply creased trousers, Wingett decided he could handle the interference and swung to do so.

"Get the hell out of here!" he ordered and started to throw a punch.

Lord Henry adopted a fighting style favored by the fast-growing school of boxers who wore padded gloves, disregarded wrestling moves, and used the three-minute round system of following the old rules. While the upright stance, foot placement and method of holding the hands looked fancy to eyes used to the old toe-to-toe, swing-and-take school, the new style proved mighty effective.

Deflecting Wingett's blow with his right wrist, Lord Henry stabbed out his left. Three times, almost quicker than the eye could follow, the Englishman jabbed his left into Wingett's face. While the blows lacked the power of a single solid roundhouse swing, their cumulative effect proved even more effective when taken with the right cross that Lord Henry whipped over to the amazed man's jaw. Shocked immobile by the three rapid, painful punches which each jerked his head back, Wingett took the fourth and shot sideways to crash into the bar.

Sharpie had turned, wanting to see the beating handed to Kerry Barran. When receiving his orders, the deputy was told that he must only intervene if it seemed the quartet could not handle things. Much as he wanted to take his part in hammering bloody revenge out of the hunter, Sharpie knew better than to disobey orders. However, the Englishman's interference gave him the opportunity he desired. Thrusting himself forward, he advanced toward the struggle.

Hearing the sound of Sharpie's rush, Lord Henry pivioted to meet the attack. He saw the badge of Sharpie's jacket and relaxed, for he retained the Englishman's respect for law and order. Out drove Sharpie's fist, catching Lord Henry full in the mouth and staggering him. Catching his balance, the Englishman slipped Sharpie's next blow, delivered a right hook into the deputy's belly and clipped his jaw with a left as he doubled over. Jerked erect again, Sharpie reeled away and tried, successfully, to keep his feet.

Turning from where he landed blows on the dazed Kerry, Potter lunged for and locked his arms around Lord Henry from behind. Along the bar,

Schmidt had recovered from his kick and hurled forward, thrusting Rixon aside in his desire to get at Kerry. Spitting blood and curses, Wingett forgot the hunter in his eagerness to take revenge on the man who hurt him, and sprang toward Lord Henry, who struggled to free his arms from Potter's grasp.

Dobe Killem knew that he must take a hand. Odds of five to two were more than anybody could manage, no matter how fancy one of them handled his fists. Before the big freighter could go to the other's assistance, he saw Sharpie halt and reach for a gun. Leaving his chair in a dive, Killem tackled the deputy around the waist and they both went crashing to the floor. In falling, Sharpie lost his hold on the half-drawn revolver and his landing threw it from its holster. Seeing the gun and noting Sharpie's hand reaching toward it, Killem swung his arm and sent the weapon sliding away across the floor to halt almost at Big Win's feet.

Still smoldering with rage at Killem's dismissal of her offer, Big Win bent and picked up the revolver. However, sanity held her enough to prevent her using the revolver as a firearm in her vengeance attempt. To do so would be cold-blooded murder and no jury could allow it to pass unpunished. Running forward, Win halted alongside Killem as he knelt astride the deputy. Her first blow with the gun's barrel landed on the freighter's head, but his hat broke most of its force. Realizing why she achieved so little, Win dragged that hat away with her free hand, then swung up the gun again. A yell of warning came to her ears, she heard the sound of feet rushing behind her, then two hands caught her by the raised wrist.

Considering their vastly different up-bringings, Calamity Jane and Lady Beryl Farnes-Grable got along remarkably well. After an enjoyable afternoon buying clothes for the trip, including a few items which Beryl wondered whether her brother would approve of her wearing, the girls rejoined the men at the hotel and had a meal. Beryl's presence prevented Calamity from going with the men when they set out to interview Kerry Barran, so the girls remained in the Englishman's suite of rooms for a time. Becoming bored, they decided to take a stroll along to see Ma Gerhity, but on reaching the hotel's lobby heard the sound of the fight and went to investigate.

They arrived just as Win took a hand and Calamity did not even wait to think before charging off to her boss's rescue. Gunbelt and whip had been left upstairs, which did not worry Calamity in the least. If she could not deal with a lard-fat calico cat using her bare hands, she ought to give up freighting and take up a seat in some ladies' sewing circle.

Darting forward, ignoring the yell of warning let out by one of the girls, Calamity caught Big Win's upraised wrist. Then Calamity jerked and swung, heaving the other girl away from Killem. Pure luck and nothing more caused Calamity to release her hold in just the right position to send Big Win reeling across the floor in the direction of the door leading from the bar into the lobby. Before Calamity could follow up her attack, Win's friend charged in, crashing bodily into the red-head and knocking her staggering. Never one to ignore a challenge, Calamity gave her full attention to handling the new assailant and found that the other could handle her end in a brawl.

Just before she reached the door, Big Win managed to regain control of her rushing body. Wild with anger at being frustrated in her vengeance bid, she wanted to take it out on somebody and was not particular who. Normally she would never have thought of offending or assaulting a well-dressed female guest of the hotel, for its owner insisted on all the courtesies being showed to his clientele on the rooming side of the business. However, in her current state of temper, Win did not give a damn what the boss wanted.

Halting her rush, she swung around a slap that rocked Lady Beryl's head to one side and staggered the blonde. Then Win realized what she had done and cold apprehension filled her. A woman as well dressed and rich-looking as the blonde would have enough pull in Otley Creek to see a calico cat who attacked her thrown into jail, or run out of town. Then Win saw an expression of fury take the place of the shock which wiped the calm regality from the blonde's face. Stepping forward, Lady Beryl hit Win. Not a gentle slap, but a round-arm swing that caught the big brunette's jaw and sent her backward. At that moment all Beryl's breeding and refinement left her, turning her into pure angry woman—than which no more dangerous creature exists. Hurling herself forward, Beryl drove one hand's fingers into Big Win's hair and with the other slashed a savage blow at the other's face. Pain shot into Win and she fought back. Spinning around, tearing at hair, Beryl and Big Win crashed to the floor to churn over and over.

Being a man with some considerable knowledge of such matters, the bartender leapt along the bar and tugged on a fancy thick tassel which trailed down in front of the big mirror's center. Decorative the cord might be, but it served a very useful purpose, being attached to a peg sunk into the wall over the mirror. The pull jerked out the peg and allowed a wooden shield to slide down along grooves until it covered and protected the Bella Union Hotel bar's prize possession. With that precaution taken, the bartender turned and hurriedy shot along the bar, scooping up bottles and glasses as he went. With all portable property rescued, he turned and gave his full attention to the fight.

Granted a momentary relief, Kerry recovered enough to last around a backhand slap that flung Rixon away from him. Avoiding Schmidt's rush, Kerry pivoted and as the German crashed into the bar, interlocked fingers and delivered a smashing blow to the back of the other's neck. Before Kerry could do more, he heard a warning yell from Lord Henry and twisted his head to learn what fresh danger threatened him. Rixon had come to a halt by a table. Grabbing a chair by its back, the small skinner rushed forward, swung up the weapon and launched a blow. Kerry twisted aside and the chair crashed into the bar, shattering its legs off. Again Kerry back-handed Rixon away and tackled Schmidt.

After yelling a warning to Kerry, Lord Henry gave thought to defending himself, or freeing himself from Potter's grasp. Before he shouted, the Englishman showed that, trained under the new-fangled Queensbury rules though he might be, he could take care of himself in a more basic and rule-free style of fighting. Even as Wingett sprang forward, meaning to take advantage of the Englishman's helpless condition, Lord Henry lashed up a right-foot kick with the ease of a *savate* exponent. Caught in the belly by the smashing impact of a fancy, well-shone boot, Wingett reeled backward with hands clawing at his middle and a desire to get rid of his last meal and drinks filling him.

Following on the kick which setted Wingett, if only temporarily, Lord Henry saw Kerry's danger, gave warning and set about freeing himself. Having witnessed the effective way in which the Englishman fought, Potter intended to hang on to a comparatively safe hold until further help arrived, so clamped hold tighter with his arms.

Down and back slashed Lord Henry's right foot, its heel catching the bulky skinner's shin bone where little flesh covered it to cushion the impact. Pain made Potter yelp and relax his grip slightly. Before it could be tightened again, Lord Henry sucked in a deep breath, expanding his chest, pressed his right hand on the left without interlacing the fingers, and forced his elbows apart. Doing so caused Potter's arms to open and loosen their hold. Swiftly Lord Henry exhaled, lowered his arms, pivoted inside the other's grasp and rammed an elbow into Potter's solar plexus. A grunt left Potter's lips and he backed off a step to catch an almost classical uppercut from Lord Henry's right fist. Before the Englishman could cut in and finish

Potter off, Wingett landed a blow to the side of his head and sprawled him into the bar.

On the brawl went, with the gandy dancers, never averse to buckling down to a fight, pitching in. Not that they took sides, but waded in at the nearest man and added a hectic quota of danger to all the original contestants. Excitement, mingled with an antipathy to the kind of woman who usually looked down on them, led the remainder of the saloon girls to join in. It might have gone badly for Calamity and Beryl had the six girls made a concerted attack, but after taking a few wild slaps, punches and kicks, they forgot their original intentions and, in some cases, revived ancient grudges, in a wild melee where one just grabbed, hit or kicked at the nearest person without regard for who she might be or what her position in life. Chairs exploded under fighting bodies, ladies overturned, glass splintered and crashed.

Attracted by the sound of the brawl, guests from the hotel and passers-by gathered at the barroom door to see what was happening. One of the first to arrive was the man who brought the cattle for sale to Corben. On the point of entering the room, he halted as he saw the fighting, threw a glance at where Calamity and two saloon girls went rolling in an all-fired tangle over a table top, grinned and remained by the door.

A gandy dancer, caught by a punch, reeled toward the door, saw Wheatley leaning with calm detachment to one side of it and rushed at him. In addition to being a mighty efficient valet, Wheatley had followed his employer into the army and held the rank of sergeant in a day when senior ranks were chosen for their ability to enforce discipline physically if necessary, rather than for educational attainments—and possessed skills not usually found in a man following such a sedentary occupation. Without dropping the watch and coat he held, Wheatley slipped the gandy dancer's punch, coming up inside it to drive his head forward. A solid click of bone on bone sounded, but Wheatley's butt sent the top of his skull cracking against the other man's nose. Dazed and agony-filled, the gandy dancer wobbled back a few steps, decided to ignore the Englishman and sought for a fresh target. His eyes focused unsteadily on the nearest of the onlookers and he made for the cattle-seller. Normally, the gandy dancer would have studied the man's six foot three of height, enormous muscular development, and avoid antagonizing him. Dazed and wild with rage, he went for the big man and launched a punch. With almost casual ease, the big man blocked the blow and shot forward his other fist. The gandy dancer appeared to fly backward, landing on the floor and

sliding under the feet of Big Win and Beryl to bring
them crashing down. Maybe he might have enjoyed being underneath two furiously struggling
women, their exposed legs threshing and flailing
before his eyes, but was in no condition to see the
attractive sight. After rolling from the man who
knocked her down, Beryl found herself in trouble.
She landed face down with Win kneeling astride
her, twisting one arm up behind her back. Sheer in-
stinctive self-preservation saved Beryl. Reaching
over with her free hand, she tried to push the fingers from the trapped wrist and rolled on to her
right side in an effort to throw the other girl off.
Inclining her body to the left to counteract Beryl's
attempt, Big Win released the wrist with one hand
and used it to slap at the blonde's head. Swiftly
Beryl flung herself over to the left, toppling Win
from her, then piled on top of her.

For almost fifteen minutes the fight raged and it
would long be discussed around Otley Creek, compared favorably with other battles of a similar nature. From the damage done around the barroom,
it seemed that Corben's plan was working; even
though the desire to see Kerry beaten to a pulp fell
far short of expectation, due to the intervention of
Lord Henry Farnes-Grable and Dobe Killem. If it
came to a point, Kerry took more than his fair
share in preventing the proposed beating once

given a chance to handle a single adversary at a time.

A table flew through one of the front windows, followed by a gandy dancer, who walked into Dobe Killem's hard right hand. Sent staggering by a kick to the rump from Calamity, a saloon girl walked into a haymaker thrown by Beryl and went out after the man. Then Beryl and Calamity returned to the business of handling the two girls who started the fuss.

At the door the big Texas cattleman caught a chair which hurled in his direction and crashed it into the chest of the thrower, Wingett, as the skinner rushed after it. Wingett reeled under the impact and a disinterested gandy dancer pushed him headlong across the room to where Kerry was engaged in altering the unlovely contours of Potter's face. Seeing another enemy approaching, Kerry pivoted into a kick which caught Wingett under the jaw, lifted him erect, spun him around and draped him unconscious across a couple of exhausted, weakly tussling girls.

Somebody crashed into the big Texan's back, bringing a frown to his face. Seeing a marshal's badge on the jacket of the man who cannoned into him while hurrying into the room, the Texan held down his annoyance. At such a moment a lawman going about his business had more on his mind than the social courtesies and could be excused for not apologizing when he bumped into a bystander.

Skidding to a halt, Berkmyer stared around him. While he expected some damage, he never foresaw a wholesale battle requiring his handling. Not that it would take much handling at that stage of the proceedings. Several men and girls lay sprawled out and most of the others looked ready to tucker off at any second. The sight of Dobe Killem sinking a punch into Sharpie's belly and dropping the deputy to his knees did not worry Berkmyer, for he and his assistant merely tolerated each other at the best of times. What dug into the marshal was seeing Kerry Barran still on his feet and, although marked up some, not battered into a wreck.

Exhausted, aching and sore, Kerry smashed a right across Potter's jaw and knocked the man flying, then the hunter slipped and went to his hands and knees. Gasping for breath, Kerry stayed down and shook his head to clear it. He heard a snarl of rage and looked up to see Berkmyer looming above him. Out lashed the marshal's foot, driving viciously at Kerry. Desperately the big hunter tried to avoid the kick. He only partially succeeded. Throwing his body aside, he moved too slowly in his exhausted state and, although saving his head, took the boot under the shoulder. Pain knifed through him and he went rolling helplessly on the floor.

Seeing the unprovoked attack, Lord Henry did not hesitate. He had just dropped Schmidt with an uppercut that threatened to stretch the German's bull neck and sprang forward. Profiting from his experience with Sharpie, Lord Henry did not allow the marshal's badge to influence him. Out shot his right in a punch which caught Berkmyer full in the center of the face, throwing him backward. Berkmyer landed rump first on the floor in the doorway. Snarling with rage, he reached for his gun.

"Leave it," ordered a drawling Texas voice, its authoritative hardness checked by the click of a cocking Colt.

Turning his head Berkmyer glared through eyes blurred with tears of pain at the speaker. First he saw high-heeled, fancy-stitched boots with good spurs on the heels; then levis pants, hanging outside the boots and with the cuffs turned back. The pants legs stretched a long way before a good quality gun-belt crossed them, an ivory-handled Army Colt in the left holster, its mate lined on the marshal with practiced ease. Above the levis a narrow waist widened to a great spread of shoulders clothed in made-to-measure costly shirt and real silk bandana. Golden blond hair framed an almost classically handsome face, while an expensive white Stetson hung back on its storm-strap. While the interfering Texan looked something of a dandy, that did not fool Berkmyer, who knew the man's name and reputation.

So did at least one other person in the room.

Shirt torn, nose bloody, bruised and sweat-soaked, hair even more wildly tangled than usual, Calamity expended some of her last energy in a wobbly right to the black-haired girl's chin and toppled her to the floor. Then, while turning to look for a fresh antagonist, she saw the Texan.

"M-Mark!" she croaked, the best she could manage in her present condition.

The action proved her undoing. An equally exhausted, tattered Win swung a wild punch at and missed Beryl but caught Calamity at the side of the jaw. Down went Calamity, landing on top of Potter, and a moment later Win crashed on top of her, knocked there by the last blow Beryl could manage. After delivering what proved to be the last punch of the fight, Beryl suddenly realized where she was, what she had been doing, and guessed how she must look, her coat gone, blouse and skirt torn and stockings in tatters. However, she had not the strength to flee from the room and sank to her knees, sobbing in exhaustion.

Chapter 6

A DISTURBED NIGHT FOR MISS CANARY

~

SLOWLY LORD HENRY LOWERED HIS FISTS AND stood gasping for breath, yet alert for more trouble. His eyes roamed around the room, seeing Killem and Kerry alone remained on their feet, then his attention went to where his sister knelt by the unconscious shapes of Calamity and Big Win.

"See to Lady Beryl, Wheatley," he said as the valet came forward. "I'll take my coat."

The hotel manager appeared, a mild little man who showed distress at the damage to his barroom, but even more so at the sight of his most distinguished guest standing with vest torn open, shirt ripped and face marked up some as a result of the fight. Spluttering his apologies, the manager came toward Lord Henry, saw Beryl and began to gobble incoherently.

"Send for a doctor, my good chap," Lord Henry interrupted. "And have one of your maids attend to my sister."

"Yes, sir, I mean your Lordship," the manager answered. "I'll have every one of those sluts jailed and run out of town for attacking——"

"I'd wait until you hear what Lady Beryl wants first," smiled Lord Henry, and looked to where Killem knelt at Calamity's side. "Is Calam all right?"

"I've seen her look better," grinned the freighter, his examination showing that no permanent damage was likely to result from the brawl. Hooking an arm under the girl, he raised her to her feet and carried her to one of the few tables left standing. "Hey, bartender, fetch me a bottle of pain killer here!"

"Sure thing, Dobe," called the man.

Before settling about the business of clearing up the fight damage, Lord Henry glared across the room in the town marshal's direction. Still seated on the floor and covered by the blond giant's Colt, Berkmyer tried to assert his authority.

"I'll jail the lot of you!" he blustered.

"You wouldn't want to bet on that?" asked the Texan, secure behind his lined revolver.

"I'll do it if I have to deputize every man in town!" Berkmyer insisted.

"Put up your gun, sir," said Lord Henry briskly, coming forward. "There will be no further need for it."

"You could be right at that," drawled the Texan and slid the Colt away.

Shoving himself to his feet and making sure he kept his hands well clear of his holstered gun, Berkmyer tried, without success, to meet the Englishman's cold gaze. Reaching inside his jacket, Lord Henry extracted a large, official-looking envelope and removed a stiff sheet of paper from it.

"I suppose you can read, my man," he said coldly, ripping open the paper and holding it toward Berkmyer.

"Sure I can read!" snorted the marshal, accepting the paper and glancing down at it. "So what's th——"

The indignation died off as he stared down at the printed heading of the paper and began to read its message. After reading only three lines, his eyes bulged out, sweat trickled down his face and he realized that he might as well forget any plans for vengeance through the law.

"I—I——" he began, then sought for a scapegoat. "If that damned hunter caused you any——"

"He did not!" barked Lord Henry. "Mr. Barran

was set about by a bunch of ruffians, after trying to avoid trouble. If anybody is to blame, they are, although I think they've been punished enough."

"Sure," grunted Berkmyer.

"And I may say I'm not satisfied with your ideas of doing your duty," the Englishman continued. "Instead of trying to level unsupported accusations, you would be better employed in organizing aid for the fighters and learning how much damage has been done with a view to obtaining payment for it.

"I'll do that," Berkmyer promised and slouched away.

Family ties and financial support were all very well; but that tall dude carried a letter requesting that all Army officers, Federal and town marshals, county sheriffs and other local authorities give him every assistance and full cooperation. Being signed by the President of the United States himself, the letter carried weight. Berkmyer did not intend bucking a man with influence going that high in the land.

Swinging away from the cold, demanding eyes, Berkmyer started to call in help to deal with the victims of the fight. Lord Henry watched the proceedings for a moment, then turned to the blond giant.

"Thank you for your timely help, sir. Of course, I doubt if the marshal meant to use his gun."

"I'd hate like hell to count on that," replied the Texan. "Best go and see how Calam's doing."

Half an hour later the Texan sat with Lord Henry, Killem and Kerry Barran in the hotel's dining room. All the men had received such medication as their injuries required and the doctor still patched up other participants in the brawl. Beryl and Calamity had been taken to the blonde's room to be patched up and even as the Texan spoke he saw Calamity enter.

Limping to the table, Calamity grinned all around and waved the men into their chairs again. On taking her seat she winced and hitched her rump up from the chair.

"Whooee!" she said. "I'd sure like to know who bit me there." She looked across the table. "How's it feel, Hank?"

"Huh?" grunted Lord Henry. "Oh, passing fair, Calam. And you?"

"Great. Apart from being all bruises except where I'm lumps. Say, that sister of yours is some gal. She's up there now telling the manager that he'd best not fire any of the gals, and she expects them to be kept off work at full pay until they're well again."

"Trust Beryl to do the right thing," smiled Lord Henry. "By the way, do you know Mark Counter?"

"I sure do," Calamity answered, eyeing the

blond giant with warmth. "Just my lousy luck. All stove-up and feeble, and Mark Counter in town."

"It'll be more peaceable for me, Calam," Mark told her.

Calamity had met Mark on two previous occasions and enjoyed each meeting to the full.* Nor did her enjoyment stem from just that fact that Mark rode as a member of Ole Devil Harding's legendary floating outfit and was right bower to the Rio Hondo gun wizard, Dusty Fog, as well as being very rich in his own right and a top-grade fighting man to boot.†

"Will you do a poor gal a favor, Mark?" the girl asked.

"Anything," he replied.

"Well, Dobe's busy right now and you know a gal daren't walk the streets after dark without a big strong man to protect her."

"So?"

"So walk me down to my wagon. I want to get my medicine bag out. That city doctor doesn't know sic 'em about curing aches got in a brawl."

"If you'll excuse me, gents," grinned Mark, shoving back his chair.

"Won't you stay and eat first, Calamity?" asked Lord Henry.

---

* Told in THE WILDCATS and TROUBLED RANGE.

† Mark's adventures are recorded in the author's floating outfit novels.

"Reckon I might manage a bit," she agreed. "A gal needs to keep up her strength for—walking to her wagon."

"I always find a good fight gives me an appetite," Lord Henry admitted.

"You should be good and hungry right now," grinned Killem. "Say, Mark, why didn't you cut in?"

"I didn't want to spoil your fun," Mark answered. "And I've got to be in one piece when I go down trail in the morning. Fact being Dusty told me I'd best come back that way."

"It pays to keep Cap'n Fog happy," chuckled Killem, and the talk drifted to stories which circulated about the exploits of the Rio Hondo gun wizard.

Food came, to be eaten with gusto; although more than one face showed signs of strain when sinking teeth into something a mite harder than a sore jaw cared to accommodate. Conversation flashed around the table and Kerry Barran found himself joining in more and more. Never since his boyhood days on the farm in Missouri had he found such enjoyable company and he made the most of it. Knowing something of the hunter's silent nature, Killem threw interested glances at Kerry and marvelled at the change.

At last the meal ended and cigar-smoke clouded

the air. Calamity finished her coffee and stubbed out the end of the cigar which she took along with the men. Giving a grunt, she stretched her arms and winced a little at the pain it caused.

"When you bunch're tired of whittle-wanging," she said, "there's a sick and sore lil gal here just dying on her feet for want of loving care."

"Come on then, Calam," Mark replied. "I'll walk you along to Ma Gerhity's place after you've collected your gear from the wagon."

On leaving the dining-room, Calamity first went upstairs and into the English couple's suite. She found the doctor fussing around Beryl, but the blonde appeared to be recovered without any serious damage or effects. So Calamity took her gunbelt and whip, wished Beryl good night, and rejoined Mark in the hall. There she also saw Big Win and watched the other suspiciously. However, it proved that Win felt no hostility and even grinned amiably.

"Say, that blonde gal's really something, Calam," Win said. "Do you know what she's done?"

"Nope."

"Squared things with the boss for us—and offered to pay for anything we had lost or damaged in the fight."

"She's a real lady and all right in my book," Calam commented.

"And mine," agreed Win. "I've told the others that anybody who tries to put the bite for more than she lost'll answer to me."

"Thanks, Win," Calamity said.

"She's playing square with us. Tell Dobe I'm sorry for hitting him."

"You tell him when he comes out of the dining-room. Maybe he'll feel like throwing a party."

Win groaned. "Right now a party's the last thing I want."

"I know just how you feel," grinned Calamity. "See you around, Win."

"Same old Calamity," Mark said, taking the girl's arm and walking from the hotel with her. "Neck deep in fuss like always."

"I tell you, Mark," she replied. "This's *one I* didn't start."

"And didn't walk two short inches to avoid, either. You'd make a hell of a wife for a man, Calam.

"If that's asking me——"

"It's not," Mark hurriedly assured her.

"You had me worried there for a minute," grinned the girl.

"You'd make a hell of a husband for a gal, too—and I should know."

The two wagons had been left at the rear of the livery barn, between the big main building and a half-circle of corrals. Pausing only to look in on hers and Killem's wagon teams, housed in one corral, Calamity walked toward the wagon, still on Mark's arm.

"Fair bunch of horses in the big corral," Mark commented. "They're some for Henry's buying, aren't they?"

"Sure. Wainer's holding them for a mustanger who caught them. Henry'll be coming down to take what he wants in the morning."

On reaching the rear of Calamity's wagon, Mark gripped her under the arms and swung her up to its bed with no more effort than shown by a nurse lifting a baby. However, before entering the wagon's covered-over section, Calamity paused and looked down at him.

"What now?" asked Mark.

"I'm scared of mice."

"So?"

"So happen I see one inside, I might scream."

"And then what?" grinned Mark.

"Just think what folks'd say happen they heard me screeching—cause I was scared of a mouse—and found you stood outside the wagon. Why it could plumb ruin you socially."

"A man has to watch his social standing," admitted Mark, and swung up alongside the girl.

Expecting to spend the night at Ma Gerhity's place, Calamity had not troubled to open out her bedroll, or take it along. Striking a match, she crossed the bare floor of the wagon and lit the lamp which hung from the roof. From there she went to the front of the wagon, knelt down and unfastened the buckles of the bedroll. A shove opened it, tarp blankets and suggans flopping out to form a ready-made bed with her war-bag in the center.

"I'm too tuckered out to walk right down to Ma's place," she said.

"So what do you aim to do?" asked Mark.

"I'd stay on here, but it's too scary for a poor, defenseless lil gal all alone."

"Reckon it would be," Mark agreed.

"A Texas gentleman ought to know the right thing to do," Calamity commented.

"A Texas *gentleman'd* go fetch a chaperone to watch over you."

"He would?"

"Surely would. Only I'm no gentleman."

"I just wouldn't have it any other way," sighed Calamity. "I'll get some of that soothing oil I got from that old Pawnee medicine woman. It sure works for stiffness and aches—if I can find some way of putting it on."

"There's always a way—happen you look," Mark told her.

The inside of the wagon lay dark, warm, and the

not unpleasant scent of the Pawnee medicine woman's soothing oil permeated the air. Snuggled up against Mark's side, Calamity awoke and felt him stirring slightly.

"Somebody just went by," she whispered.

"I heard them," Mark replied and rolled free from the blankets.

Range habits caused Mark to retain his trousers, even though removing his shirt when he went to bed. He reached out, drew on the shirt and then slid the right-hand Colt from its holster. Moving with just as much speed, and in equal silence, Calamity slipped into her shirt, but laid her defensive emphasis on the long bull whip rather than her revolver. Side by side, they moved to the rear of the wagon and Mark drew up the cover to let them look out.

"Down by the big corral gate!" Calamity breathed.

A quarter moon gave them just enough light to make out the dark shape which made its stealthy way along the side of the big main corral. Swiftly Mark swung himself over the tail gate of the wagon, dropping soundlessly to the ground. Wise in such matters, he tossed the Colt from his right hand to the left on landing. He figured he might need the gun, but wished to avoid becoming an open target.

No man sneaked in a suspicious manner toward

the gate of a corral containing valuable unbranded horses at night if he had innocent intentions. With the penalty for horse-stealing being death, it did not pay to take chances at such a moment.

At least two people walked by the wagon and only one of them made his way toward the corral gate. However, Mark did not have time to look for the other. Already the man had reached the gate and fumbled with its fastenings. Once the gate opened, the sound of shooting would spook the remuda and allow it access to the open range. So Mark had to prevent the gate opening if he could; and chance the second man not being in a position to interfere.

"Hold it!" he snapped.

A snarling curse sounded from the man at the corral gate and he whirled to face Mark. Flame spurted from the man and lead slapped the air close to Mark's body. The blond giant did not hesitate. Up slanted his Colt, its hammer falling as his powerful forefinger depressed the trigger. Although partially blinded by the muzzle-blast, Mark heard the distinctive sound of lead striking human flesh. Even before he could move from his position, another shot crashed out; this time from the side of the corral. Only one thing saved Mark. Unable to see the blond giant against the background of the wagon, the second horse-thief aimed at the

Colt's flame, sending his bullet to where a right-handed man ought to be. Mark held his Colt in the left hand, which made enough difference to save him.

Calamity saw the second shape just an instant too late to warn Mark, or stop the shot being fired. Springing forward, she shook loose the whip's coils and let fly at the very limit of its range as time did not permit her to go closer. Specially made for her, the whip's lash was lighter than usual, but no shorter; and the slightly thinner lash proved no less effective than would its heavier male counterpart. Nor did it lack accuracy, as was proved by the screech which followed on the rifle-crack of the whip in action. Caught by the very tip of the lash, the man felt as if his face had burst into flames. He gave a scream, let his gun fall and turned to flee. Calamity let him go, not knowing that he had lost his gun. While a mite reckless at times, she was no fool and knew better than to go chasing an armed, desperate man when carrying only her whip; effective weapon though it might be. Instead, she swung around and gave her attention to the horses in the corral.

Spooked by the shots, the remuda milled around restlessly. Mark ignored the light which appeared at one of the barn's windows and dashed toward the corral gate. At any moment one of the frightened horses might hit and force open the gate, then the whole remuda would stampede. If that happened, Lord Henry's hunt would be delayed until fresh mounts could be gathered in.

Hurdling the still shape sprawled out on the ground, Mark landed by the gate and thrust it closed just as one of the milling horses struck it. He had heard the shot, crack of Calamity's whip and scream, so did not expect any further trouble from that side. Swiftly he slammed home the gate's bolts and then looked around.

"Are you all right, Calam?" he called.

"Sure. How about you?"

"I'll do." Mark assured her, then grinned as he wondered what the livery barn's owner would make of his and Calamity's barefoot and untidy appearance.

Chapter 7

A NIGHT FOR MAKING PLANS

~~~~~~~

"I DON'T WANT TONIGHT TO INFLUENCE YOU IN any way, Kerry, or have you under the impression that I think you're beholden to me," Lord Henry said after Calamity left on Mark's arm. "But if you feel like changing your mind, my offer is still open. I would like you along as my guide."

"I'd near on decided to go before they jumped me," Kerry answered. "Seeing the way you can fight didn't weaken me any."

"Then you'll accept?"

"Sure will."

"Look, we can't stay on down here. I see the waiter giving us 'Why-don't-you-go-to-bed?'

looks. Let's go up to my suite and have a natter about this and that, shall we?"

"You're the boss," Killem agreed.

Watched by a relieved waiter, who had seen too many late-hours sessions develop to miss the signs, the three men rose and walked from the room. On the way upstairs, a thought struck Kerry.

"Your sister will be asleep," he said.

"She's a heavy sleeper," Lord Henry replied. "Especially after tonight. I bet she's stiff in the morning."

"Calamity's got something that'll cure it if she is," Killem remarked. "I hope she's enough of it for all of us."

Wheatley stood in the sitting-room of the suite when the men entered. "The doctor has left, my Lord, and her ladyship is sleeping. I've put the drinks on the table ready for you."

"*Three* glasses?" commented the surprised Kerry.

"I've seen too many hunting gentlemen not to know the signs, sir," Wheatley explained. "Your face told me you would accept Lord Henry's offer."

"Don't you want to play poker with me, friend?" warned Kerry.

"No, sir," Wheatley replied seriously.

"I'd like you to look over my battery, old chap," Lord Henry remarked. "And don't look so surprised, Wheatley's always doing it. Come on over and see if I'll need anything more in the gun line."

Crossing the room, Lord Henry unfastened the reinforced leather box. Its top and front side both opened and exposed eight guns securely racked in two rows. At the peer's side, Kerry could hardly hold down a whistle of admiration. With two exceptions, the guns in the case showed the superb workmanship for which Britain in the mid-1870s was famous.

Reaching into the case, Lord Henry freed and took out the uppermost gun. He held it out for Kerry to study the short twin barrels, superbly carved woodwork and general excellence of its design and construction. The gun showed signs of considerable use, but not abuse.

"It's a fine piece," Kerry admitted, "but I like longer barrels in a shotgun."

"So do I," agreed Lord Henry. "But if you have longer than a twenty-four-inch barrel, an eight-bore rifle weighs too heavy for use."

"That's a rifle?" asked Kerry, staring at the twin muzzles, each larger than the mouth of a ten-gauge shotgun.

"Of course. William Evans made it for me. I first used it while elephant hunting in the Transvaal. It stopped a charging bull with over two hundred pounds of ivory in its tusks."

"I reckon it'd stop near on anything," Kerry conceded. "Can I——"

"Of course," Lord Henry replied, breaking open the rifle and showing its empty barrels; an elementary precaution taken instinctively.

Despite its somewhat squat appearance and heavy weight, Kerry found that the rifle possessed such superb balance that it snapped naturally to his shoulder and handled with the ease of a top-quality shotgun. Glancing along the rib between the barrels, over the V of the backsight to the blade of the foresight, Kerry wondered what sort of sensation went with shooting a rifle that had a larger caliber than most shotguns he had seen.

"It's a touch heavy," he said, returning the rifle.

"You only notice that until you touch off your first bullet," Lord Henry answered. "With twelve drams of powder shoving eleven hundred grains of lead out, you need something to absorb the kick—not that even sixteen pounds of gun stops it all, but the weight helps."

"Yeah," grinned the hunter. "Say, this'd be hell to shoot lying down."

"Only ever knew one chap who tried."

"What happened to him?"

"The recoil broke his collarbone."

"How'd you use it then, Henry?" Killem inquired.

"Standing up, shooting off-hand. Of course, you won't get accuracy at anything like two hundred, or even a hundred yards. But you don't pop off at an elephant or buffalo at that range anyway. When either a tusker or a Cape buffalo comes at you with blood in his eye, you really need something that will stop him in his tracks."

"I've never yet been charged by a buffalo," Kerry remarked.

"There's a difference between a Cape buffalo and one of your bison, Kerry—you don't mind if we dispense with formalities, do you?"

"I reckon not, Henry. How're they different?"

"I've photographs of——"

"The album is here, my lord," intoned Wheatley, materializing with a large, leather-bound book in his hands.

While the two Americans examined photographs of what, to them, were strange animals, Lord Henry unpacked the rest of his battery. In addition to the big bore, he had three Express rifles, one .577 in caliber and the other two .405, a brace of magnificent Purdey twelve-gauge shotguns, a Remington Creedmoor single-shot rifle and a Winchester Model '66 repeater, both new-looking compared with the worn condition of the others. He handled the guns with loving care, as befitting the old and trusted friends all but the two

American guns had proved to be. While removing and checking the battery, he answered questions about the various pictures which aroused his companions' interest.

"That's a man-eating tiger from the Assam Valley of India. Killed fifty natives and two white chaps who went after it. Gave me the devil of a time before I finally bagged him."

"How about this critter?" Kerry inquired. "I never saw a bull with horns like that afore."

"You wouldn't have. That's a Cape buffalo and he gave me some of the worst moments of my life. Some blighter had wounded him and left him alive. Pain drove him mad, but didn't make him act stupidly. When he took to terrorizing the natives, he had to be stopped."

"Just take a look at that elephant, Kerry," breathed Killem, tapping one photograph. "I sure as hell never saw one that size in any travelling circus."

"You wouldn't. They use Indian elephants, but no man has ever trained an African elephant. I needed that big double when he came at me."

Kerry sat entranced as the pages of the album turned. Some of the animals he had read about, a few he had seen in travelling circuses, many were unknown to him. The more he saw, the more he knew that the lean, tanned Englishman and he shared the same interest in life. Lord Henry Farnes-Grable took far more pleasure in matching his wits against a really fine specimen than in shooting inferior or average creatures. Taking him out ought to prove real interesting.

From what Lord Henry said, Kerry realized that the other knew much about all aspects of hunting. Without boasting, the peer told of his hunts and the listening men guessed that he left much of the actual hardships and danger unmentioned in his clipped, to-the-point stories.

"How about my battery, Kerry?" he asked.

"I don't know what you'll need the eight-bore for," the hunter answered. "Grizzly, maybe, but you don't need that much gun to drop a buffalo—one of our kind, that is."

"It wouldn't be a hunt without it along," Lord Henry explained. "We might find a use for it."

"How about the others?"

"These are Evans' Express rifles," Lord Henry explained. "Beryl uses one of the .405s, and she's a pretty good shot. They make pretty good second guns. After all, a chap out after sport doesn't want to use a big bore all the time, especially on the small stuff."

"How'd they shoot?"

"Well enough up to around three hundred yards. Although I must admit that the combination of a heavy powder charge and light bullet leaves much to be desired in the killing line. Chum of mine took a shot at a tiger and the bullet burst apart when it hit the blighter's skull. Dazed it somewhat, which wasn't exactly the idea. Anyway, I bought the Remington for long-distance work."

"It's a straight-shooting gun and carries well," Kerry admitted. "What happened to your pard?"

"Luckily he had an eight-bore along. When the tiger bounced up and charged, he shot it from a range of eight feet. I must say that he stopped it that time."

"I reckon he would at that," grinned Killem, eyeing the wide mouth of the Evans big bore.

"I bought the Winchester for saddle work and in case of fuss with the Indians," Lord Henry went on, "Although I hope I don't have to use it for that."

"We shouldn't have any trouble with them in the Wind River country. It's Cheyenne land and they've been peaceful, sticking to the treaty since Sand Runner got put under about eighteen months back," Kerry replied. "You was on the wagon train that got him, wasn't you, Dobe?"

"Sure was," agreed the freighter. "One way and another, it was quite a trip, too."

"The Indians won't trouble us, with luck," Kerry went on, deciding to hear the full story later.

"Not that we'll take any chances with them. How about spare horses?"

"I've fixed for some to be brought here. They're down at Wainer's livery barn and we can pick from them in the morning."

"We'll need a skinner to take care of the hides," Kerry said. "Old Sassfitz Kane, the hound-dog man, can skin, but he'll be needed to handle the dogs."

"That's soon arranged. Frank Mayer offered to loan me his skinner, cook, horse-wrangler and camp help if I could find a reliable hunter—and I've done that, Kerry. I'll have Wheatley shoot off a telegraph message in the morning."

"Then we've got about all we need," commented Kerry, wondering if Frank Mayer would regard him as a suitable man to handle his trained team of assistants. "I suppose you've got enough ammunition?"

"Two hundred rounds each for the rifles, three hundred and fifty shotgun shells, reloading tools," answered Lord Henry. "I suppose we can get powder and lead in town?"

"Sure. Corben stocks the best imported English powder and has lead——"

The crack of revolver shots chopped off Kerry's words, coming through the window Wheatley opened to allow fresh air in and tobacco smoke out. Thrusting back his chair, Kerry rose, crossed the room and looked out into the night. Like most sharpshooters, he learned to gauge accurately where a sound originated, and he felt he could make a shrewd guess at the source of the shooting. While revolver shots were not a novel sound around Otley Creek, hearing them late at night demanded investigation.

"Down by the livery barn, I'd say," he told Killem as he joined him.

"Yeah," agreed the freighter. "Reckon we'd best go down and take a look."

"I'd take it kind if I could borrow a gun, Henry," Kerry said, knowing that the combination of shooting and the livery barn might make armament necessary.

"Take the Winchester," Lord Henry answered, going to the gun case and extracting boxes of bullets. "You'd best have a shotgun, Dobe."

Which did not imply a lack of trust in the freighter's knowledge of weapons. Kerry knew the workings of a Winchester repeater, but Killem had never used a twin-barrelled rifle. Learning how to handle such a weapon in the heat of a gun fight would not be practical or sensible.

Each of the trio carried a loaded weapon when they left the hotel room and hurried through the streets in the direction of the livery barn. One thought ran through each mind, the safety of the horses. Without them, the trip could not be taken.

On arrival at the rear of the livery barn, the three men saw that their fears were groundless. Already a small group of citizens stood in the background, lanterns illuminating where Mark Counter, Calamity Jane and the owner of the livery barn stood at the edge of the corral, a body sprawled close by. Calamity and Mark had found time to dress fully before the arrival of the first of the townspeople and Wainer had been too concerned about his horses to notice their appearance when he came on to the scene.

"Howdy, Kerry," Wainer greeted. "It's Siwash Jones. Mark there stopped him."

"Looks like he finally got ambitious and died of it," Killem grunted, knowing the dead man to be a poor-spirited drunkard who hung around Otley Creek making out as best he could.

"Looks that way," agreed Wainer. "He didn't make shucks at it like everything else he turned his hand to. That Texan was walking Calamity home when they saw Siwash and another jasper down here. The other one got away."

"We can't win them all," drawled Killem, overlooking the fact that Calamity and Mark had left the hotel long before the time of the shooting. "Did you lose any of the stock?"

"Nope. Which's real lucky for me. I'm holding them for the owner, and if they'd gone he'd expect me to make good the loss."

"Strikes me as funny, though," Kerry put in. "Siwash trying something like this. Sure he'd steal, given half a chance, but nothing as valuable as a whole bunch of horses."

"He stinks of rot-gut whisky, worse than usual," Wainer replied. "Most likely that's what did it."

At that moment Marshal Berkmyer made his appearance, scowling around and ready to make a big show of keeping the peace. He turned hate-filled eyes in Kerry Barran's direction, noticed and gave a polite—if not friendly—nod to Lord Henry, and then demanded to be told what all the fuss was about.

"Now me," drawled Mark Counter, "I'd say that was obvious."

"So Siwash tried to steal the horses, huh," sniffed Berkmyer, ignoring the blond giant's lack of respect. "Who shot him?"

"I did," Mark replied. "His gun's there, one chamber fired, and you'll likely find the bullet-hole in Calamity's wagon."

"Ain't doubting you," answered Berkmyer in a tone which showed he would like to do so but dare not. "He asked for it."

"Sure he did," agreed Calamity. "But why'd he do it?"

"Huh?" grunted the marshal.

"I've seen him around town enough times to know he didn't have the brains or guts to try anything this big. Why'd he try to run off the remuda?"

"Those hosses arc valuable," Berkmyer pointed out.

"Sure. Too valuable for him to take."

"He's drunk."

"He'd have to be real drunk to get up enough guts to try it," Calamity insisted. "Even if that drunk, he would think about doing it."

"Maybe the other feller put him up to it," Mark suggested.

"What other feller?" asked Berkmyer, looking around him with more interest than the possible sight of a second horse-thief should warrant. A hint of relief showed on his face when he failed to see another body. "Where is he?"

"Took off running," Calamity answered. "I carved a smidgin out of his face with my whip afore he went though."

"Which 'ought to make him real easy to find," Mark drawled.

"Yeah," agreed Berkmyer, although he did not sound convincing. "It should at that."

While Mark knew little about local conditions, what he had seen since his arrival did not fill him with faith in Berkmyer's ability as a lawman. In fact, his views on the marshal, although accurate and correct, were not charitable to Berkmyer. Mark would be considerably surprised if the other ever located and arrested the second of the thwarted horse-thieves.

"Where do you aim to start, marshal?" he asked.

"I'll bet it's some drifter, new to town, got Siwash all stirred up and set him to it," answered Berkmyer, confirming Mark's belief that he would always take the easiest way out of any difficulty.

"I'll just bet it was," sniffed Wainer, who had been close enough to overhear the words. "Town's full of drifters who know that I've got a corral-full of unbranded hosses and know where they can sell 'em."

"What's that mean?" Berkmyer demanded.

"Nothing at all. Did your cousin say he'd made me an offer on my place?"

"Any reason why he should?"

"None as I know of," admitted Wainer. "Only if those hosses had gone, I couldn't pay the feller who caught them without selling out."

"Are you hinting at something?" growled the marshal.

"Just talking is all," replied the barn's owner calmly. "Say, didn't Siwash do some swamping and heavy toting at times for Corben?"

"Did, and for near on every other place in town as long's they'd put up with him. Corben fired him out today because he never turned up for work sober."

"Maybe needed extra money then," drawled Mark. "Losing his job and all."

"Sure," agreed the marshal. "And he'd be ripe for an offer to make some. If I can find the feller who talked him into helping, it'll clear up a whole heap of things around here."

"One thing, marshal," Mark said quietly.

"Yeah?"

"I brought four men in with me. Not one of them needed money and I'm telling you that they wouldn't steal. When I ride out of here tomorrow, I aim to take them with me."

"You'll do it, too, as long as they're not involved," Berkmyer promised, seeing one chance of quietening suspicions drop away.

In many a town along the railroad, a cowhand could be framed for crimes and killed without arousing hostility among the local citizens. Berkmyer knew that any attempt to do so in this instance meant facing Mark, and that he did not intend to do.

"Everything appears to be all right, marshal," Lord Henry remarked, coming from where he and Killem had been inspecting the freight teams. "Can we help you in any way?"

"There's not much to do, it being dark and all," Berkmyer answered, grabbing the opportunity to change the subject. "Do you aim to have a guard on the corral all night, Wainer?"

"Sure," agreed the barn owner, "If I can find anybody to do it."

"I'd say that would be your job, marshal," Lord Henry commented. "You or one of your men."

"I don't have but the one deputy and he's stove up from the fight," Berkmyer answered sullenly.

"It's on your head," warned the peer. "But I expect to find those horses there in the morning."

"Don't fret, they will be," snarled the marshal, thinking of the letter carried by the Englishman.

If looks could kill, Lord Henry Farnes-Grable would have died at that moment. However, Berkmyer raised no objections, although he did not relish standing guard all night, especially as he doubted if any other attempt would be made to remove the horses. Yet if he failed and the remuda went—well, he knew the Englishman possessed the necessary social contacts to cost him his post as marshal. After ordering that the body be removed, he looked up at the sky. At least there did not appear to be any sign of rain.

"Dang spoil-sport," said Calamity, her voice pitched so that only Mark caught the words. "Now I'll have to go to Ma's place for the rest of the night."

"He sure is one obliging marshal," Mark replied. "Real smart, too. He knew that feller had been drinking——"

"That didn't take smart thinking," objected Calamity.

"It did the way he did it," Mark said. "He knew without going anywhere near the body—and that's what some folks might call smart."

Chapter 8

A LADY TAKES TO THE SADDLE

"GREAT SCOTT, BERYL," LORD HENRY ejaculated, staring at his sister as she entered the sitting-room of their suite. "Where did you get those clothes?"

Considering that Lady Beryl wore a Stetson hat perched on her head, bandana knotted at her throat, man's shirt and levis pants, and high-heeled riding boots, his surprise had some foundation. Beryl smiled at her brother's reaction.

"Calamity and I bought them yesterday. She said they would be more suitable than my riding habit for when we're on the Great Plains."

"Then you should have waited until we got to

the Plains before—oh, well, have it your own way. You usually do."

"Thank you, dear," Beryl replied and stretched. "I don't know what that oil Calamity used on me was, but it's taken all the stiffness out. When do we look over the horses?"

"As soon as we've breakfasted, so let's make a start."

Despite her bold front, Beryl felt just a few qualms as she approached the door to the hotel's dining-room. Her clothing did not fit as snugly as Calamity's outfit, but still exposed considerably more of her shape than convention allowed. With Calamity, completely at ease in the revealing men's clothing, the feeling had not been too bad. However, Calamity left after arriving early to apply the soothing oil to Beryl's aching frame, and the blonde wondered what people might think of her appearance. Then a thought struck her and she smiled. Taken with the blackened eye and scratched cheek gained in the fight, and her activities the previous night, she doubted if her appearance would cause too much comment.

Her guess proved to be correct. After a long, searching glance at her, the few people using the dining-room returned to their eating. Letting out a slight sigh, Beryl sat down and made a good breakfast.

On arrival at the livery barn, Beryl and Lord Henry joined Calamity, Killem, Kerry and Mark—the last-named being introduced to Beryl by Calamity.

"Well," Killem said to Beryl, "what do you reckon to them, ma'am? Wainer here says they're the best he's had through his hands in years."

"I've never yet met a horse trader who didn't," smiled Beryl, and Wainer took no offense, but grinned back. "May we look them over more closely?"

"Feel free, ma'am," Wainer answered.

One horse took Beryl's eye as soon as she walked to the side of the big corral. Although nothing showed on her face, she knew that she must have the paint gelding as her personal mount. It might not be the biggest horse in the remuda, but that deer-red and white gelding conveyed an impression of alertness, intelligence, speed, agility and stamina that pleased Beryl more than she could say.

"Which one do you like?" Calamity asked as Wainer returned to talk with Lord Henry.

"The skewball."

"The *what?* Oh, you mean the paint. Sure, he's the one I had my eye on."

"Let's start having them out, old chap," Lord Henry suggested.

"Any particular one first?" inquired the barn's owner innocently.

"*You* trot them out how *you* like," countered the peer, too old a hand to be caught in such a manner.

Grinning, Wainer looked to where two of his men stood ready to start work. That dude might talk fancy, but he sounded like he knew horse-trading. It showed in his refusal to pick out a specific animal which might have caught his eye, allowing the seller to adjust the price accordingly.

"Bring out that dun," ordered Wainer.

Mounting the corral rails, one of the hired men swung his rope and sent its loop sailing forward in a nearly perfect hooley-ann throw to head-catch the required horse. From the way in which the dun allowed itself to be drawn in peaceably, it knew what the manila rope about its neck meant.

Giving the horse a quick but thorough check, Lord Henry nodded his approval. "Looks all right," he said cautiously. "Trot it up and down for a time, so I can see if its legs fall off when it moves."

After a brisk trotting and walking back and forward, during which all four legs stayed firmly in place, Lord Henry was satisfied. The dun looked up to carrying weight, had the build for speed and staying power. Nor did it show any undue signs of distress when Kerry fired off a shot from his carbine close by.

"I'll take that one," the peer stated.

"Hello," Beryl suddenly remarked, swinging away from watching her brother examining the next horse to be led from the corral. "I certainly didn't expect to see one of you out here."

Turning, Calamity saw Shaun approaching. The big wolfhound had been left at Ma Gerhity's place, but must have got out and trailed its master to the barn. To Calamity's horror, Beryl walked toward the dog. Having a shrewd idea of how Shaun would react to such a liberty, Calamity reached for the handle of her whip, ready to use it to protect Beryl from an attack. Already the big dog had come to a halt, standing on rigid legs, tail stiff and unmoving, his top lip curling back to expose the upper canine fangs in silent warning.

"Watch him, gal!" Calamity hissed, realizing that a sudden yell might make Beryl start back and precipitate Shaun's attack.

She did not need to bother. All Beryl's life had been spent in and around the country and she knew better than to ignore the dog's warning.

"All right, I understand," she said quietly, and looked in Calamity's direction. "He's a beauty and as well bred as any I saw in Ireland."

"You mean there's more like him?" asked Calamity.

"Irish wolfhounds? I've seen several of them, both in England and Ireland, and this one is as good as any. I wonder who owns him?"

"I do. Miss—ma'am——" Kerry put in, having seen his dog's arrival and come to protect Beryl if she should be foolish enough to go too close. His words died off as he could not decide how a Lady should be addressed.

"Why not say 'Beryl' and avoid confusion?" the blonde smiled. "I hope you are taking him with us, Kerry."

"I sure am, Mi—Beryl."

"Good, then I'll have a chance to get to know him better."

Something about the girl's attitude told Kerry he did not need to waste time giving warnings. She knew enough about dogs not to make any fool mistakes like trying to pet Shaun; and he still had work to do. Telling the dog to settle down and keep from underfoot, Kerry rejoined Wainer, Killem and Lord Henry. While doing so, he noticed Potter's bunch among the crowd of loungers who gathered—as such always did whenever anything out of the ordinary happened—to watch the selection of the horses. It seemed that the quartet had been on the point of leaving town, for their mounts stood in the background, bedrolls on the cantles. Kerry doubted if the four would cause him any trouble, especially as he now wore his weapon belt and carried his carbine.

Horse after horse came out, to be examined, accepted or rejected. At last the paint came from the corral and passed into those selected to be used on the hunt. Beryl walked forward as the paint was led toward the group at one side.

"I'll take him, Henry," she announced.

"He's only been three-saddled, ma'am," Wainer warned and, seeing the girl did not understand, went on, "that means the breaker's only ridden it three times. That'd be enough for a man to handle it——"

Such a remark was calculated to rouse Calamity's ire and brought an angry snort from her.

"Toss a saddle on him, one of you," she said. "I'll give him a whirl."

Grins crossed Mark's and Killem's faces, for both knew Calamity to be better than fair at handling a snuffy horse. Certainly the paint did not appear to have more than average cussedness and Calamity ought to be able to take the bed-springs out of its belly, especially as it had already been three-saddled.

Mark collected his girl's saddle from her wagon while Killem led the paint into the breaking corral which had been left empty for the purpose of testing any horse selected out of the remuda. Handled by two such skilled men, the saddling went by without a hitch and at good speed. From the calm manner with which it accepted the indignity, the paint knew better than to fight the inevitable—which did not mean it would allow itself to be ridden without protest.

Mark's huge bloodbay stallion and Kerry's gray stood saddled and ready for use at one side of the breaking corral. When dealing with range horses that had been kept in such close confines for a time, it paid to have the means to catch any animal that broke away.

After checking everything was to her satisfaction, Calamity swung astride the paint. Mark continued to hold the horse's head until she settled down firmly in the saddle. Then, at her command, he released his hold and retreated hurriedly.

At first the haste did not seem necessary, for the horse remained standing patiently. Calamity decided to force the issue and rammed her heels into the paint's ribs as an inducement to movement, and immediately had her wish granted. Bogging its head, the paint blew up with a series of high, back-arching jumps; impressive to watch, but nothing out of the ordinary. Always one to enjoy being in the limelight, Calamity had hoped for a better chance to show off her skill.

In the course of her lifetime, over-confidence had

landed Calamity in more than one scrape, and so it proved that day. Suddenly the horse made a fence-corner pitch, going up pointing due north but landing at a forty-five-degree angle to its original direction. Taken by surprise, Calamity felt herself slipping and took the easiest way out. Kicking her feet from the stirrup irons, she parted company with the saddle in full flight. She had ridden for long enough to learn how to fall and, although lighting down on her rump, softened her landing in a manner which saved her from serious injury. Bouncing twice, Calamity slid halfway out of the corral almost at Mark Counter's feet."

"Thought I saw you on that horse, Calam," the blond giant remarked.

"Help a lady up, you long, white-topped slab of useless Texas cow-nurse!" she answered hotly, "I'll show him who's the boss next time on."

Before Calamity could do so, Beryl ducked between the fence rails. Shooting out his hand, Lord Henry caught his sister by her arm.

"Don't be silly, Beryl!" he snapped. "You've not ridden astride since we were children."

"Haven't I?" smiled Beryl. "It's time I learned if I still can, then."

With that, she shrugged his hand from her arm and walked toward the horse. Speaking gently, she reached for and caught hold of the paint's reins.

Just as smoothly, she moved around until in a position to mount. Up went a dainty foot and into the stirrup iron. Then, with a little swing, Beryl mounted the horse. Her move was so smoothly executed that she had her rump on the saddle and other foot firmly in iron before the paint realized that another human being challenged it. Once the realization came, the paint took off in a high buck. Although she rose into the air more than the horse, and her face showed pain as she landed, Beryl stayed in the saddle instead of dirtying her shirt on the ground.

While the saddling took place, Kerry led Shaun into the livery barn and left him there. To a certain degree Shaun could be trusted around people, but Kerry preferred not to take chances. Already an excited crowd gathered round the corral, and in the excitement somebody might kick or bump against the wolfhound with unpleasant and painful results. After safeguarding the public, Kerry hurried back to see Calamity thrown and Beryl take the red-head's place.

Again and again the paint bucked, leaping high and slamming down hard; but without the devastating change of tactics which sent Calamity out of the saddle. Yells of admiration, whoops of delight and shouts of advice rang out from the men who surrounded the fence. From the excited way some of them acted, Kerry showed wisdom in removing his dog.

"Yahoo!" Mark whooped, almost deafening Calamity at his side. "Stay up there, Beryl!"

"Damn It!" Calamity snorted, feeling just a touch of pique at Beryl's success. "She didn't get bit where I did last night."

"I bet she got more sleep, too," Mark grinned.

"*You're* to blame for that," Calamity reminded him. "All I—watch him, gal, he's going to pitch fence-cornered."

And the horse did, using the trick which threw Calamity. For a moment it seemed Beryl would smell corral dirt. She hung over in the saddle, made an effort and remained in her seat. Pique forgotten, Calamity almost drowned out the cheers of approval at Beryl's skill.

"Where did Ber—your sister—learn to ride like that?" asked Kerry, turning to Lord Henry.

"I'm blessed if I know," the peer admitted. "Probably been riding astride back home when nobody watched her."

"She's sure some gal," enthused Kerry. "I've only seen——"

His words chopped off as he saw the paint change tactics. Forgetting bucking after its lack of success, the horse ran across the corral, heading for the fence facing the open range beyond the town. By that time Beryl had gained the feel of her mount and found no difficulty in staying on it at a gallop. However, she knew that she could not turn the paint in time to avoid a collision with the fence. Feeling the horse's muscles bunch, she guessed what it planned and gave the idea her full cooperation. Hand, legs and body worked in conjunction with the paint as it took off, rising up toward the top of the six-foot-high top rail of the fence. Spectators scattered hurriedly and a concerted gasp rose from among the others as the paint sailed into the air.

Having ridden to hounds on numerous occasions in England, Beryl knew how to take a jump; but she had never done so while sitting astride. So when the paint landed, she instinctively adjusted herself to take the impact as when riding side saddle. Although she managed to retain her seat, the paint's landing slammed her down hard enough to make her lose control of the reins for a vital instant. Taking the bit between its teeth, the paint bolted, streaking away from the corral and toward the open range.

Even before the girl reached the stallion, Kerry raced forward and went afork his gray with a flying bound. He lit down with feet digging into the stirrups and started the horse running in almost the same move.

"Watch those horses!" Mark shouted, for in the excitement and confusion Wainer's men ignored the animals selected to accompany Lord Henry on the trip and they showed signs of spooking.

Running to his horse, Mark jostled Calamity aside and swung into the saddle. His example brought the attention of other men to Lord Henry's stock and helped to prevent it scattering.

"Come on," Potter growled to his companions, throwing a glance in the direction taken by the fleeing paint and pursuing gray.

"What's up?" Wingett mumbled through a swollen jaw and mouth.

"Barran's just left town and we're going after him."

"Why?" asked Rixon.

"To get what's coming to us. He's carrying money on him and that gray'd bring a fair price from some Army officer."

While broke, having been fired for their failure on returning to Corben, the other three showed no great eagerness to tangle with Kerry Barran again. True, he would have enough money on him to make the effort worth while, but they all knew the risks involved.

"He'll have that limey gal with him," Wingett pointed out.

"Sure, but not that damned dog," answered Potter. "Let's get after them and if there's a chance, we'll take him."

Having no alternative plan, and being under the marshal's order to get out of town—neither Berkmyer nor Corben wanted the quartet to be around to answer awkward questions—Potter's companions followed him to their waiting horses. Nobody gave them a glance as they mounted and rode out of town, headed at a tangent to the direction taken by Beryl and Kerry.

Mark's prompt action prevented the scattering of the horses from being too serious. Already they had become split away from each other, but he turned back a couple and then more men came up. Calamity threw open the gate to the corral which housed her own and Killem's teams, using the cracking of her whip to keep the animals already inside from leaving. Used to the explosive cracks of the bull whip, the team horses did not need touching with its lash to remain obedient to its wielder's will. After the horses had been corralled, Calamity turned and looked out across the range. Such was the broken nature of the land that Beryl and Kerry had already passed out of sight.

"Reckon we'd best get after them?" she asked.

"They'll be all right," Lord Henry replied. "Beryl can ride well enough and Kerry will catch up with her before she gets too far away."

"I dunno," objected Calamity. "That paint had a fair head start and it's carrying less weight than Kerry's gray."

"You trust old Kerry to fetch her back in one piece, Calam," Killem comforted. "The country's a mite rough, but that paint's been raised in stuff like it and's too smart to run blind. Look how it took that fence."

"There's that," the girl admitted, knowing a panic-stricken horse would have smashed bodily into the fence instead of going over it.

"You sound concerned for Beryl's welfare, Calamity," smiled Lord Henry.

"So I should be," she replied, then grinned back. "That's my saddle she's using."

"Oh, well," drawled the peer, "if it doesn't come back, I'll buy you a new saddle."

Just as Calamity sought for an adequate reply, she noticed certain absentees from the crowd. Taken with the departure of Kerry Barran, she did not like the idea of not seeing Potter's bunch present.

"Hey," she said. "Those four yahoos who jumped Kerry last night were here."

"So I saw," Lord Henry replied. "I don't think we'll see any more of them."

"You're right at that. They've gone."

"If you mean Potter and that other bunch who

used to skin for Kerry," Wainer put in, "they just now rode off."

"Which way?" Mark asked.

"Down to the South-West, thought maybe they're headed for the forward construction camps, them not working for him any more."

"Could be nothing to it," Mark said doubtfully.

"I'd sure hate to count on it," Calamity answered.

"Those blighters wouldn't dare do anything while Beryl's with Kerry," Lord Henry objected. "But I hate to take a chance. I say, Mr. Wainer, I'd like a saddle if you have one."

"Make it two," Calamity corrected.

"Are you coining along, Calam?" asked the peer.

"Sure am," agreed the girl. "We'd best have some of your horses, Wainer. There's not time to take bed-springs out of that bunch in the corral."

"Good thinking, gal," Mark said, knowing that using the horses from the corral would cause a far longer delay than taking mounts from the barn's hire-supply.

Crossing to the barn's door, Calamity opened it and looked to where the big dog came to its feet. She tried to hide the apprehension that rose as Shaun walked in her direction. One wrong move would see her badly bitten, that she knew.

"Easy there, boy," she said quietly. "I'm not fixing to touch you. All I want to do is get you after your boss."

Shaun walked by Calamity and across to where he had last seen his master. Dropping his head, he sniffed around, sifting through the mingled scents until he located the one he wanted. Watched by the girl and men, the big dog followed on Kerry's line to where the hunter mounted. For a moment the sudden disappearance of his master's scent picture fooled Shaun. Then he picked up the scent of the gray, which he knew well enough. Swinging on to the gray's line, he loped away in the direction the horse took when chasing after Beryl's paint.

"I feel better now," she said.

"And so do I," Lord Henry admitted. "Come on, Calamity, let's get the horses and ride."

Chapter 9

A NICE DAY FOR KILLING

~ ~

AT FIRST BERYL FELT JUST A LITTLE AFRAID AS THE
horse tore out of town with her on its back. Not
blind panic, but merely a normal fear which could
be kept under control. With the bit firmly between
its teeth, Beryl had no way of stopping the paint.
However, she soon found that it did not rush
blindly along, endangering itself and the rider. Instead it ran as a wild animal fleeing from something unpleasant, fast but alert for anything which
might cause it to injure itself. The speed at which
the paint ran made falling off its back impractica-
ble; even if Beryl had considered taking that way
out. Not that she did, coming from a stock which

did not lightly flinch from danger. Once she knew that the horse was not in a wild blind flight, she settled down to keep her seat and enjoy the ride.

Kerry urged his gray after the paint, but soon knew he could not close the gap on the lighter-loaded animal until it tired. Booting the carbine, he concentrated on keeping the gap between them from enlarging and followed ready to lend a hand should Beryl find herself in difficulties.

On they went, tearing out over the rolling, open range. Kerry could not help admiring the girl's riding skill, especially when the paint went down a steep incline. Bounding out at the bottom, the horse lit down running. For a moment Beryl tilted dangerously, but by that time she had adjusted herself to riding astride and found no difficulty in regaining her seat. Dropping from his saddle, Kerry slid down the slope alongside the gray and remounted when they reached the bottom.

Not for three miles did the paint show any sign of slackening its pace. At last Kerry called up a burst of reserve speed from the gray and drew alongside the paint. He expected to see fear or concern on the girl's face; but read only exhilaration and excitement as she flashed a surprised but delighted smile at him. Edging his gray closer to Beryl's mount, Kerry leaned over. He reached out and his fingers closed on the paint's head-stall.

With a firm grip on the other animal, Kerry slowed his horse and brought both to a gradual halt.

"Are you all right?" he asked and jumped to the ground.

"Fine," she replied, eyes sparkling and bosom heaving. Tossing her right leg across the saddle, she slipped down and landed before the hunter. "I *was* a little frightened at first, but that soon passed. Then when I found he wasn't running blind, I sat back and enjoyed the ride—not that I could have stopped him."

Turning, she ran a hand along the horse's lathered neck. Without needing any instructions, she set to work cooling down the paint. After watching her for a moment, Kerry decided she could manage and attended to the gray.

"You must think I'm an absolute horror, Kerry," Beryl remarked, when the horses had been cooled down and they prepared to walk some of the way back to town.

"Why should I, ma—Beryl?"

"Well, last night I became involved in a brawl. Then I appear this morning dressed like this——"

"What's wrong with the way you're dressed?" asked Kerry.

"It's hardly a costume a lady should wear in public," Beryl smiled. "Not that I've been acting very lady-like recently."

"I've seen a few ladies in my time. Not for-real ladies like you, though. Can't say any of them dressed that way, but I don't care."

"Is that a compliment?"

"It was meant to be. Most of them ladies would've screeched if they saw a mouse and couldn't tie their shoes without help. Can't say I took to them. You're not like that."

"I try not to be," Beryl said. "Of course, I've been on hunting trips with my brother before and am used to roughing it. But I never dressed like this."

"Once we get moving, you'll damn—sorry, ma'am, you'll near on live on a horse. They clothes'll be better than a fancy dress then. Reckon we'd best start heading back to town."

"What kind of horse is this, Kerry?" Beryl asked, indicating the paint.

"Just a range mustang. You'll see plenty of them running wild on the Great Plains. Come from Spanish critters that escaped way back, so a railroad surveyor told me, with a mixing of blood from stuff that escaped or got lost from wagon trains."

"Are there many of them?"

"I've seen herds of hundreds."

An interested gleam came in Beryl's eyes. "Doesn't anybody try to catch them then?"

"Sure," Kerry answered. "The Indians pick up what they want. A few fellers make good money picking up herds, breaking them and selling them."

"All good horses like this paint?" the girl breathed.

"Nope. He's an exception. You don't see many that good."

"But they have stamina and an ability to stand off local diseases. Crossed with blood stock, they could be turned into ideal mounts for this country."

"That's strange. I was just thinking the same thing last night."

Leading their horses and discussing the possibility of improving the range-raised mustangs' bloodline, Beryl and Kerry walked side by side across the rolling country in the direction of the town. Ahead the land dipped and rose in folds and valleys; outcrops of rocks and clumps of trees or bushes dotted the slopes and valley bottoms. Ideal country for an ambush, although Kerry, absorbed in conversation on an interesting subject, overlooked the fact.

Potter and his men had been unable to keep the departing riders in sight after they left town, but followed the tracks of the two racing horses. Unsure of how long the paint would run, or which route Kerry might take back to town, the quartet separated and fanned out in a line to cover as much of the range as possible. In the center of the line, Potter caught sight of their prey first, signalling to Rixon and bringing the small man over. However, they could not attract either Wingett or Schmidt's attention. Potter would have preferred to bring all four of them together, but as he studied the situation, decided they were better off split up. Concealed among a fair-sized clump of bushes, he and Rixon appeared to be in direct line with Kerry and the girl. Off to the right Wingett left his horse hidden and inched his way through cover on a course which ought to bring him close to where the couple passed. Over on the left, Schmidt halted behind an outcrop of rocks, drew his rifle and covered where the big hunter and girl ought to go by. The two flank men had moved ahead some thirty yards, forming what might be termed the lips of the funnel down which their victims must travel.

"There he comes," Rixon snarled, holding his rifle in sweating hands.

"Hold your voice down!" Potter hissed. "That damned hunter's got ears like a bobcat."

With that Potter looked for a place where he might rest his rifle and still keep concealed. In addition to having keen ears, Kerry Barran had eyes like a hawk and used them constantly when on the range.

Loping along on his master's trail, Shaun covered the ground with the almost tireless gait gained by long hours of exercise. He could not track at the same speed the horses galloped, but kept up a fair pace. Faintly, carried by the wind, he caught the scent of his master and knew he drew close. Then another scent came, almost blocking out that of his master. Deep and low rumbled a snarl in the dog's throat as he recognized the body odor of two of the men who had been around so much and whom he hated. In addition to the smell of unwashed bodies, mingled with dried blood and general filth, he caught the unmistakable aroma of hate and hunting. Quickening his pace, the dog lifted his head from the tracks and ran on the wind-carried scent.

"I've got him lined up," Potter breathed. "Don't shoot until he's between Wing and Smitty. Let's make good and sure of him."

At that moment both heard the rapid patter of feet and rustling of the bushes, followed by a deep, rumbling snarl. Twisting around, Rixon saw the huge dog burst into sight and uttered a shriek of warning. Potter started to turn, recognized the danger and jerked his rifle around. Its barrel struck a branch and held, causing his finger to jerk the trigger. Flame tore from the rifle's barrel, but its bullet tore harmlesly through the trees.

Leaving the ground in a smooth leap, Shaun hurled at Potter. The burly man tried to tear his rifle free from the branch, released one hand and raised an arm to defend his throat. A numbing, burning sensation drove into the arm as Shaun closed his powerful jaws on it. Snarling in fury, the dog bore Potter backward and to the ground.

Rixon staggered backward, fear on his face as he stared at the struggling man and dog. The big wolfhound had always been a source of terror to the skinner and he realized that, unless he did something fast, a recurring nightmare where Shaun jumped him might come true. Jerking out his revolver—having dropped the rifle at the first sight of the dog—he fired a shot. Shaun yelped, jerked and flopped sideways to the ground.

"My arm!" moaned Potter, rolling hurriedly away from the dog and clutching at his injured limb.

"I'm getting out of here!" Rixon croaked and ran for his horse.

For a moment Potter glared at the dog, wanting to batter its still body into a bloody wreck. Then he, too, turned and made for his mount. Pain beat through him, knifing out from his arm. Only with an effort did he manage to drag himself into the saddle, then he clutched at the horn with his good arm and urged the horse after the departing Rixon.

All too well both men knew how Kerry Barran felt about his dog. Most likely the shot came soon enough to prevent him from riding into Wingett and Schmidt's ambush. In which case the hunter stood a good chance of escaping. He would find his dog's body and the Lord help the man who shot the wolfhound when Kerry Barran laid hands on him.

So, without a thought for their companions, Potter and Rixon fled in the direction of Otley Creek. Topping a rim, they saw riders approaching in the distance, recognized them, and changed direction rapidly. To be trapped by Dobe Killem, Calamity June, Mark Counter and that fancy-talking English dude meant being held until Kerry Barran arrived, and neither relished the thought. So they headed off across the plains, and might have felt relieved that nobody followed them.

For once in his life, Kerry Barran lost his habitual caution when out on the open range. Walking along with the girl, he missed noticing certain signs that ought to have been obvious to him—and would have been at any other time.

The first hint of danger came when a shriek sounded from a large clump of bushes about a hundred and fifty yards ahead. Then Kerry heard a familiar roaring snarl, saw one of the bushes shake violently and a rifle cracked out. Again the bushes shook violently as if something heavy thrashed about among them. A revolver barked and Kerry caught the sound of his dog's yelp of pain. However, by that time he had other troubles.

In a single instant after hearing the first sound, Kerry reverted to his normal, keenly alert self. Over to his left he located a patch of unnatural color and a closer inspection showed it to be Wingett's shirt. Not that Kerry gave a thought to the skinner's choice of clothes. What interested the hunter was how Wingett lined a rifle in his direction.

Hooking an arm around Beryl's waist, Kerry lifted her from her feet and bore her to the ground. Her squeak of protest and amazement died as she heard a rifle shot and saw Kerry's hat whisked from his head by a close-passing bullet. In bringing Beryl to safety, Kerry released his gray's rein and she lost her hold of the paint. Startled by the shot and sudden movements, both horses continued to move on. Although neither went far before their trailing reins brought them to a halt, the gray carried Kerry's carbine well beyond his reach.

Not far from where Kerry and the girl landed on the ground lay a small dip. Still holding Beryl to him, Kerry rolled over her body, swung her up and across him so that they passed down the incline and out of Wingett's sight.

A snarl left Wingett's lips as his prospective victim disappeared. However, he had been in a position to see the carbine in the gray's saddleboot and knew the big hunter never carried a revolver. Ignoring his single-shot Ballard rifle, Wingett drew his revolver and charged through the bushes toward where Kerry disappeared. While covering the fifty yards which separated him from his victim, Wingett wondered if his bullet caught the hunter. Maybe nothing more than a body's convulsions carried the couple out of sight. Even if Kerry Barran still lived, his carbine remained in plain view.

Just an instant too late Wingett remembered the Indian fighting-axe Kerry always carried. Even as the thought, shocking in its realization, formed, the skinner reached the top of the dip. He halted, staring down, frozen by the memory and understanding of his danger, staring to where Kerry faced him, standing in the attitude of just having thrown something.

Once in the dip, Kerry rolled clear of the girl. His hand flashed to the tomahawk and slid it free. Taken from a raiding Sioux war chief, the fighting axe had been produced by a man with a fine idea of what such a weapon should be. It was made from real good steel—most likely bought from a trader who wanted to come back, and so sold worthwhile goods—honed to a razor edge and perfectly balanced for slashing chop or skilled accurate throwing.

Kerry heard the crashing rush of Wingett's approach and realized what the other planned. Having worked with the skinner for some time, Kerry possessed a fair idea of how the other thought. Trust Wingett to take the most obvious way out.

"Keep down!" Kerry ordered, having already rolled from the girl, and came to his feet.

Right foot advanced, Kerry gripped the axe in his right hand and looked up the slope. He measured the distance with his eye and swung up his arm, keeping the axe's cutting edge aimed straight at where he guessed Wingett would appear. Back and forward Kerry swung the axe, just a couple of times to make sure it lined up correctly. There would be little or no time to correct his aim once the man appeared, but Kerry's keen ears told him just where Wingett would come into sight. Timing his move just right, Kerry wound up and swung his arm forward in a powerful sweep which propelled the axe through the air even as Wingett's head top showed over the rim. Turning over once in its flight, the axe streamed toward the skinner. A screech of terror broke from Wingett's lips. He tried to throw up his arm and ward off the hurtling missile, but left the move too late. Razor-sharp steel bit into flesh and the axe's weight carried it deep into the side of Wingett's throat. Blood spurted as the steel sliced through the jugular vein. Wingett's scream chopped off and he stumbled backward out of sight, his rifle and revolver dropping from his hand.

Beryl saw the axe leave Kerry's hand and realized what it was meant to do. Swinging her head away from the sight, a movement caught the corner of her eye. On looking fully around, she saw the big shape of Schmidt among the rocky outcrop about seventy yards away. Even as she watched, the man raised a rifle and lined it in the direction of Kerry's back. Beryl did not hesitate. Stepping forward, she placed her body between Kerry and the rifle.

With his sights lined on Kerry's broad back, Schmidt was on the verge of squeezing the trigger when the girl stepped into his line of fire. Knowing his ability with a rifle, the German did not care to chance hitting the smaller mark offered by the hunter's head. Nor did he want to shoot the girl, relying on the bullet passing through her and into Kerry's body. From what he had seen and heard, Schmidt knew the ambush plan had gone wrong and that he most likely stood alone on whatever he did. While the hunt for Kerry Barran's killer might not be pressed too hard, the same did not apply should the girl fall victim to a murderer's bullet. The killer of any woman could expect to be hunted down without mercy and relentlessly. That particular woman's killing would be even more so if Berkmyer told the truth about the amount of political and social pull her dude brother commanded.

There had been a stormy meeting earlier that morning when Corben demanded to know why his plan to force Kerry Barran back to work failed. Everybody involved tried to lay the blame on somebody else and one excuse offered by Berkmyer concerned a letter carried by the dude and signed by the President. Like Berkmyer, Schmidt had no intention of antagonizing folks whose influence went *that* high.

Having reached his decision, Schmidt lowered the rifle. From his position on the rocks, he commanded a good view of the surrounding range and saw the distant riders who scared off his companions. Realizing that he could not expect so many friends to be riding out of Otley Creek, Schmidt knew he had better not delay his departure. Already Potter and Rixon fled and he dropped to the ground, took his horse, then rode off in the opposite direction to the other two. A lone man made less tracks than three and any pursuit would tend to follow the larger group. There were no ties of loyalty to hold the German with Potter and so he did not worry about being separated.

Bounding forward, Kerry caught up Wingett's fallen revolver. A better shot with a rifle, he might have taken the Ballard but guessed that it was empty. Gun in hand, he moved cautiously up the slope. The sound of hooves brought him swinging around and he saw Schmidt riding off. He wondered why the German had not fired. Realization burst on him as he remembered how Beryl moved behind him. At the moment he had thought she did it for protection. Now he knew that it had been him she moved to protect.

"What a gal," he thought. "She'd make a good wi——"

He chopped off the thought unfinished as he recalled who and what Beryl was. A woman of her birth and breeding would want better out of life than a foot-loose hunter who lived by his skill with a rifle; and would not want him entertaining such thoughts about her. Even if she did have tender feelings toward him, the sight of Wingett sprawled on the ground and bleeding his life away would chill them off quick enough.

"Stay down there!" he ordered. "And keep your head down."

"Of course," Beryl replied, her voice cool and calm.

Bending down, Kerry gripped the axe's handle and plucked it from Wingett's neck. Nothing could save the man, in fact, even as Kerry removed the weapon, Wingett died.

"May I come up, please?" Beryl called. "I heard your dog yelp. He may be injured and need our assistance."

"He might at that," agreed Kerry. "Go the other w——"

Before he could finish, the girl came up the slope to his side. She sucked in a sharp breath and walked past the body, back straight—almost ramrod stiff—face rigid. Following the girl, Kerry wondered what she must think about him.

"I had to do it," he said.

Beryl bent down and picked Kerry's hat from the ground. For a moment she held the battered hat, then poked a fingertip into the bullet hole. "I know," she said. "He meant to kill you."

On handing over the hat, her fingers brushed against Kerry's and her eyes met his. He read no revulsion or condemnation in the girl's expression—but what he saw jolted him to his toes. If any other woman had looked at him in such a manner, he would have known what to do. With Lady Beryl Farnes-Grable, sister of his employer, Kerry could not bring himself to answer her eyes' message.

Almost angrily he jerked his hat on to the rusty

brown hair and walked to where the horses stood range-tied by their trailing reins. Beryl watched him go, a mingled smile and frown on her face. Then she gave her head a shake and followed on his heels. Catching their horses, they mounted and rode side by side, but in silence, toward the clump of bushes.

"Shaun!" Kerry growled, anguish in his voice, as he saw the dog lying sprawled on the ground.

Flinging himself from the gray, Kerry strode toward the dog. Before he reached its side, Beryl had run by and dropped to her knees, a hand going to the bloody furrow across the dog's head.

"He's not dead!" she gasped, relief plain in her voice. "Get me some water, Kerry, I want to bathe the wound."

While unslinging his canteen, Kerry studied the wound and knew what had happened. Whoever shot the dog came within a quarter of an inch of missing. The bullet just nicked Shaun in passing, creasing the scalp and knocking the dog unconscious. Even as he looked, a shudder ran through Shaun's powerful frame and the dog stirred slightly.

Placing her hat crown upward on the ground, Beryl told Kerry to pour some water in. Using her handkerchief, after stifling his objections to wetting her Stetson, she bathed the graze and Shaun rolled into a lying position

"Move away from him," Kerry ordered.

"I'll have some more water," she answered, emptying that already in the hat. "Easy now, boy, we'll soon have you on your feet again."

A growl began in Shaun's throat, but the girl never moved or took the hand from his back. Keeping her voice quiet and soothing, she talked to the wolfhound and her hand stroked his back. Kerry poured out the water, watching for the first hint of an attack. Placing the hat before the dog, Beryl steadied him as he sat up and began to drink. After a time Shaun raised his head and looked straight at the girl. A cold feeling of anxiety ran through Kerry as he watched. Then he saw the dog's tail wag and Shaun lowered his head to lick Beryl's hand.

Chapter 10

A TIME TO MAKE FINAL PREPARATIONS

~~~

THE PARTY FROM TOWN APPROACHED AT A FAST trot, guns out ready for use, horses being held down to that pace so as to have a reserve of speed should pursuit be necessary. Relief showed on Lord Henry's face as he saw his sister safe and well. Dropping from his saddle, he walked toward where the girl knelt at Shaun's side.

"You're all right, dear?" he asked.

"Yes," she replied, her hand on the dog's neck. "But I wouldn't come any closer if I was you."

Noting the dog's warning altitude, Lord Henry halted, so did Calamity, who had been following on the Englishman's heels. Admiration, tinged with a little exasperation, showed on the red-head's face as she saw that Beryl had made friends with the wolfhound.

"Well dog-my-cats!" Calamity said to Beryl. "If you're not a living wonder. If anybody else'd tried to touch that fool dog, he'd've chewed their fingers off plumb up to the armpits."

"It's all done by kindness," smiled Beryl. "A gypsy taught me how to do it."

"Did she teach you how to ride as well?" grinned Calamity, too warm-hearted and generous of nature to hold a grudge against somebody who showed talent.

"That runs in the family," Lord Henry told her. "It and scaring one's friends out of their wits."

"Good Lord!" Beryl gasped in mock surprise. "Did my nipping off like that worry you?"

"Well, Calam did express concern at you being on her saddle when you went; and I suddenly realized that you've the keys to our strong box at Lloyds."

"And I thought they chased after me for myself," sighed Beryl. "Shaun, it's nice to know that you still love me."

"Heard some shooting," Calamity remarked, becoming serious.

"Those chaps Kerry had the trouble with last night tried to ambush us," Beryl answered.

"Who was it, Kerry?" Mark was asking at the same time as Beryl told her story to Calamity and Lord Henry.

"Potter's bunch," the hunter replied. "I had to kill Wingett."

"It looks like you did," said Killem dryly, directing a pointed glance at the hole in Kerry's hat. "What happened?"

"Looks like they followed me out of town. Laid for me around here. Rixon and Potter were up here. Shaun jumped one of them. Figure it was Potter, or old Shaun'd be dead now. Rixon creased his head with a bullet and they took to running. The other two hid out down that ways. Wingett cut loose and missed, but Schmidt run without shooting."

"It was close," drawled Mark, realizing that much of the story remained untold. "I reckon that big cuss saved your life."

"Him and Beryl both," agreed Kerry, and told of the girl's actions.

"That's one smart and brave gal," commented Killem. "And just look at her standing there alongside Shaun."

"She's got a way with animals," Kerry said.

"She's got a way with folks, too," grinned Mark. "You ask Big Win." His face lost its smile. "Why'd they jump you, *amigo*?"

"Looking for evens after last night, most likely."

"And why'd they jump you last night?"

"I'd cost them some money," Kerry replied, and explained the circumstances, finishing, "That wouldn't set well with them."

"Do you reckon Corben set them up to kill you?" asked Killem.

"Nope," Kerry answered. "He might have told them to jump me and work me over until I agreed to go back hunting for him, but he'd not want me dead. That way I'd be no use to him."

"Want us to take out after them?" Mark inquired.

"No. They'll be gone and I don't reckon I'll see any more of them. We'd best tote Wingett's body back to town though."

"Dobe and I'll tend to it," Mark promised.

At that moment Lord Henry walked over. "Thanks for saving Beryl, Kerry."

"She saved me, too," Kerry replied. "I'm only sorry she saw what she did."

"It wasn't your choosing that those thugs tried to kill you," the peer said. "You'll find that Beryl doesn't hold it against you."

"I hope not," Kerry answered, and something in his tone brought the peer's eyes to his face. "Let's take the ladies back to town."

"And the body?"

"Dobe and Mark'll tend to that."

Accepting Kerry's reply as the best solution, Lord Henry mounted his horse. Accompanied by Kerry, the peer escorted the girls back in the direction of Otley Creek. For a time none of them spoke much, then Kerry brought his gray to a sudden halt and stared off to the north.

"Well I'll be damned!" he ejaculated.

The other three also turned their eyes and followed the direction of his gaze. On a distant slope a number of small black dots moved slowly into view and downward. Of the three, only Calamity knew what the dots were and she felt a little puzzled at Kerry's surprise.

"What are they?" asked Beryl.

"Buffalo," Calamity answered. "You'll see plenty of them on the plains."

"But not this close to town, the way they've been hunted down," Kerry objected. "It's a bull and his bunch of cows."

"Mind if we ride over and take a look, old boy?" Lord Henry inquired.

"You're the boss," Kerry drawled. "I see you brought a rifle along."

"The others insisted I collect it before we came after you," Lord Henry replied, glancing down to where his .405 Express rode in its saddleboot. "I'm not keen on taking a buffalo, unless it's really good."

Steering the others along a route that kept them out of plain view, Kerry made his way toward the herd. As an aid to his skin-hunting, he had studied the buffaloes' habits and wondered what caused the herd to keep on the move at a time when they would normally be grazing.

"Can't get in much closer on the horses," Kerry said at last. "If we leave them down in that hollow, we can move in on foot."

"I think I'll stay with the horses and Shaun," Beryl remarked.

"And me," Calamity agreed. "I've seen all the buffaloes I need."

"Have it your own way, girls," Lord Henry smiled. "You ladies usually do."

"Now there's what I call a real smart man," Calamity grinned.

On reaching the bottom of the small hollow, Kerry told Shaun to stay and swung from his saddle. He drew the carbine from its boot and looked to where Lord Henry slid out the Express. Leaving the girls, dog and horses, the two men advanced cautiously on foot toward the approaching buffalo.

The herd continued to move slowly along its original course, some dozen or so cows of the same general size and, at one side, an exceptionally big old bull. It towered inches higher than the cows, with massive horns that brought a low whistle of admiration from the big hunter.

"Just look at those horns," he told Lord Henry.

"Are they something special?"

"You might say that. I've seen a fair number of buffalo and those are the biggest pair of horns I've ever come across."

"Is there any chance of my bagging him?"

"Reckon that Express'll stop him."

"If I'm close enough."

"We'll move down to that bunch of bushes at the foot of the slope then."

"Where'll be the best place to hit him?" asked Lord Henry before moving.

"Right smack between his two eyes," Kerry replied.

"That would spoil the head for mounting," Lord Henry pointed out.

"Then you'll have to wait until it swings and get it just behind the shoulder. Aim about halfway down and you ought to hit the heart."

"And if he doesn't——"

At that moment another bull topped the slope over the advancing herd, chopping off Lord Henry's words as it stood for a moment and gave out a deep guttural roar. Swinging around, the herd bull faced the other and gave vent to a bellow in answer to the newcomer's challenge and then moved to the rear of the bunch of cows.

While not quite as large as the herd bull, the newcomer packed a fair amount of size and weight; it also appeared to be somewhat younger. To the watching men, it seemed that the herd bull showed some reluctance at turning to meet the challenge. The reason for the herd's continuous movement now became obvious. Having beaten off its younger challenger, the herd bull tried to leave it behind and avoid another clash. At last the younger bull caught up and prepared to resume the battle, bawling out a challenge that must be accepted.

Down the slope thundered the younger bull, giving vent to the whistling hiss Kerry knew so well. Sounding like steam rushing through the safety-valve of an overheated engine's boiler, the charge whistle of the attacking bull shattered the air, mingling with the deep grunt of the older animal which advanced to meet the attack. Both bulls carried signs of previous engagements, open wounds giving mute testimony to a mating battle that had been carried on intermittently for the past eighteen hours.

Using the momentum built up in the downhill charge, the younger bull crashed into the elder and forced it backward. Although the herd bull kept its feet, the challenger drove it back on to the level ground at the foot of the slope. For almost twenty minutes the two bulls charged, butted and hooked at each other. Standing clear of the fracas, the cows showed no interest in the contesting males and grazed unconcerned.

More than once during the fight Lord Henry could have taken a side-on shot at the herd bull but made no attempt to do so. He would never have even thought of taking such an unfair advantage. Instead, he and Kerry stood and watched a primeval struggle for mastery.

"The old one's losing," Lord Henry breathed.

"Looks that way," Kerry agreed.

Head to head, the bulls strained against each other, hooves churning the earth and sending it flying. Slowly the herd bull gave ground and, sensing its rival weakening, the challenger thrust with renewed vigor. Reeling under the extra force, the herd bull turned away from the challenger. Instantly the younger bull lunged, slamming full into the other's side and hooking savagely. Staggering from the impact, the old bull turned and fled, bellowing dolefully. After giving chase for a short distance, the young challenger and new leader of the herd swung back to claim his spoils.

In its attempt to avoid the pain of its rival's attack, the old bull headed straight for the clump of bushes behind which Kerry and Lord Henry had hidden on halting to watch the fight. Still bawling pitifully, as if knowing its days as herd leader had ended, and trailing thick blood behind it, the old bull rushed blindly into the bushes, smashing through as if they did not exist.

"Look out, Kerry!" Lord Henry yelled, diving to one side while the scout flung himself in the other direction.

On landing, Lord Henry swivelled around and threw up his Express. As the fleeing bull buffalo burst between the men, he fired left and right, aiming the shots just behind the shoulder and in the center of the body's depth. The bull's legs buckled on the impact of the bullets and it crashed to the ground some feet beyond the two men. Instantly Lord Henry broke open the Express, thumbing out its empty cases and replacing them with two loaded bullets from his jacket pocket.

"Good shot," Kerry said admiringly, and meant it. "Reckon you'll need them?"

"I'd say he was done for," Lord Henry answered. "Only there's no point in taking chances. Chappie I knew did, walked up to a lion he'd shot and the blighter got up just as he reached it. Hadn't bothered to load his gun first. They say he still had the annoyed expression on his face when they buried him."

Kerry glanced at the Englishman's sober face and caught the twinkle of humor in his eyes. It seemed that Lord Henry was not the aloof, unsmiling man he gave the impression of being. Nor did he lose his opinion of the peer's hunting savvy while watching the cautious manner in which the other approached the bull. Although the precautions proved unnecessary, neither man regretted taking them.

"Twenty-six inches at least," Kerry remarked, trying to sound nonchalant and hide the excitement he felt. "I've not seen many as big and damned few bigger."

"That's how I like them," Lord Henry replied. "We'll have to arrange for the head-skin to be collected."

"I'll tend to it," promised Kerry. "He'll be tougher'n an old Sioux moccasin to eat, but the marrow bones'll still be tasty. Tongue shouldn't be too bad, either."

At that moment the two girls rode up, each leading a horse and with Shaun loping alongside Beryl. Dropping from her saddle, Beryl studied the bull for a moment, then turned to her brother.

"He's a beauty, dear. I think we'll have his head mounted between the tusks from the big bull elephant you took in the Transvaal."

"I thought of replacing Aunt Agatha's portrait over the fireplace with it," grinned Lord Henry. "But I don't think she'd go much for the idea."

"I *know* she wouldn't," Beryl replied. "What do you think, Calam?"

"I'd hate like hell to try eating him," answered the practical Miss Canary. "But I reckon our two hunters know what they're doing. Only I states now that they'd best come up with something a whole heap younger once we hit the plains happen they want to keep me happy."

"That we'll do," Lord Henry promised. "I'll stay here while the rest of you go to town and send out the means to move the trophy in."

"There's no need for that if you lend me your jacket," Kerry replied.

Without arguing, Lord Henry removed his jacket and passed it to the hunter. Kerry went to the buffalo and hung the coat so that it swung and swayed from the horns.

"Will that work?" asked Beryl.

"Sure will," Calamity assured her. "Them turkey buzzards up there and the buffalo wolves won't come near for a fair spell as long as it moves."

With the precautions for safeguarding the trophy taken, the party rode back to Otley Creek. On reaching the hotel, they found Dobe Killem standing on the porch and Calamity needed only one glance to warn her that the freighter had something on his mind.

"Have Frank's men arrived yet, Dobe?" Kerry asked.

"Come in on the westbound. I've sent them down to Ma Gerhity's."

"Going to need the skinner and your wagon."

"You've got trouble here, Kerry," warned Killem quietly.

"How's that?" Kerry asked.

"Corben's putting it about that you never paid for the last load of supplies and claims he aims to have you held for debt."

"He does, huh?" said Kerry gently, and dropped from his saddle, drawing the carbine as he landed.

"One moment, Kerry!" barked Lord Henry. "That's no answer."

"I figure it's a right smart one," Kerry replied.

"It is—if you want everybody to believe Corben's telling the truth."

"I've never lied to any man, 'cept about hunting, and that's not lying," Kerry growled and swung away from the party.

Tossing a leg across the saddle, Calamity lit down on the ground and swung free her whip.

"You just stand fast and listen to Hank, Kerry," she ordered. "Just try walking away and you'll do it on a broken ankle."

Nothing he had heard or seen of Calamity led Kerry to believe she might be making an idle threat. That whip in her hands possessed the power to do just what she said and she knew how to handle it so as to achieve the desired result. Even so, he might not have stopped. His eyes met Beryl's and found them quizzical, yet holding an expression which clearly said their future relationship depended on how he acted.

"You've got a right good argument, Calam," he said.

"That's better," Lord Henry stated. "*We'll* go and see Corben now."

"That jacket won't keep the wolves and buzzards off the buffalo forever," Kerry warned. "Its head might be ruined."

"Blast the head!" Lord Henry barked. "There'll be others."

But not many with such a size of horn, as all the party knew. Beryl smiled at Kerry, letting him know that she approved of his decision. "If you wish, dear, I'll accompany the skinner. Perhaps Calam will come along?"

"Sure I will," agreed Calamity. "I reckon old hot-head here won't go shooting up the whole danged town. Say, where's Mark?"

"Gone to tell his boys they'll be staying on for another day. The town's been giving a party to honor their distinguished visitors," Killem explained. "I reckon you and M—Lady Beryl'll attend, Henry?"

"Of course," Henry agreed. "But let's get this business with Corben settled first, shall we?"

"Yeah," Kerry agreed. "Let's."

Just a touch of nervousness crept through Corben as he saw Kerry Barran enter the store. Not even having Berkmyer and Sharpie hovering in the background made him feel any more secure as both had failed to handle the big hunter. Behind Kerry came Dobe Killem and that damned dude Englishman. Worse than that, the railroad's depot agent stood at the tobacco counter being served, and brought the presence of an independent witness into the affair.

"Hear tell you want to see me, Corben," Kerry said, his carbine under the crook of his arm. "Where's Bernstein?"

"Huh?" grunted the startled storekeeper.

"I paid him for the stores and watched him enter it in your books."

"The book's right here," Corben answered, waving his hand to a thick ledger on the counter top. "But there's no record of your payment in it."

"Where's this Bernstein chap?" Lord Henry put in.

"He left town on vacation."

"I saw him go, mister," the agent put in. "Looked like he was heading down track to find a dentist, way his face was bandaged."

Exchanging glances with his companions and seeing they also caught the significance of the words, Lord Henry turned to Berkmyer. "Have you any interest in this matter, marshal?"

"Only to keep the peace."

"Including serving a warrant on Mr. Barran?"

"If I have to," Berkmyer agreed.

"Which also entails gathering all witnesses?" Lord Henry went on and the marshal nodded. "Then you must arrange for the speedy return of this Bernstein chap."

"I don't know where he's gone," objected Berkmyer.

"Telegraph the police in each town along the railroad," suggested the peer. "If that does not bring results, hire the Pinkerton Agency."

"And who pays for it all?"

"The one who loses the case, if I know anything about the law."

Apprehension bit into Corben at the words. He knew that the Pinkerton Agency possessed the means to locate and return Bernstein, no matter where he went, even if some town marshal along the track did not pick him up. Once returned the reason for his facial bandage would be learned.

Toothache did not make it necessary—as Corben well knew.

"One other thing, marshal," Lord Henry said, having watched the storekeeper's expression and chosen his moment perfectly. "Could you tell me the name of a general store in the next town along the track. I wish to buy supplies for my hunting expedition."

"I've everything you'll need, sir—my Lord," Corben pointed out in his most ingratiating manner.

"Under the circumstances, I hardly feel it advisable to do business with you," Lord Henry answered. "I might discover that payment for my goods was not recorded by your clerk."

Give him his due, Corben knew when to call a game quits. Nothing he could say or do would induce Kerry Barran to work for him again. He decided to give up his efforts and forget revenge, if doing so brought him the Englishman's business.

"Waldo!" he called to his second clerk. "You were here when Mr. Barran paid for his stores?"

"Yes, Uncle Cyrus," Waldo agreed, catching on with remarkable speed. "I remember Bernie didn't mark it in the book. Told him about it, too, and he said he would. He must have forgotten to do it."

"That's what he must have done," beamed Corben. "I'm sorry about all the trouble this has caused, Mr. Barran."

"We all make mistakes," Lord Henry remarked, jabbing Kerry hard in the ribs before the hunter could raise any objections. "Of course, Mr. Corben will make a public announcement that gives the full facts."

"Sure I will," Corben agreed, willing to do anything if it brought him a sizeable order.

"And I think you'll admit he can supply us with everything we'll need for our trip, Kerry?" the peer went on.

"Sure he can," Kerry answered grudgingly. "Maybe better than any other store closer than Chicago."

"Then here is where we'll buy the supplies," decided Lord Henry. "Dobe, if you'll stay here, I'll send Wheatley along with my list and you can attend to it."

"Sure enough," grinned Killem.

"That will leave you and I free to make the final arrangements, Kerry," the peer said. "I know Mr. Corben wants to make an adjustment to his books and we'll not prevent him from doing so."

"Huh?" grunted Corben, then the light glowed. "Oh, sure. These darned young clerks. You can't rely on them to do anything properly."

Not until Corben had recorded Kerry's payment did Lord Henry offer to leave. Outside the store, Kerry swung to face the Englishman.

"Damn it, that bandage around Bernstein's face could mean that he was the one Calam caught with her whip last night."

"It could also mean that he had toothache," Lord Henry answered. "Which is how we'll leave it. There's nothing we can prove and the marshal wouldn't want to try. Come on, let's see that chappie with the hounds. With luck we can pull out tomorrow afternoon."

Chapter 11

A TROPHY WELL EARNED

~~◆~~

AFTER A BUSY AFTERNOON SELECTING AND LOAD-
ing supplies, followed by a hectic evening at a din-
ner and ball thrown by the citizens of Otley Creek
for their distinguished English visitors, the party
managed to roll out the following day. Calamity
felt a few pangs of regret at separating from Mark
Counter, but sustained herself with the knowledge
that their paths would most likely cross again.

For the first two days they passed through country well, if not over, hunted by the Otley Creek
men. From the third morning animals began appearing in ever-increasing numbers. While used to
the variety of animals offered on the plains of

Southern Africa, Lord Henry found no cause for complaint at what he found. Although not yet gathered in their vast seasonal migration herds, buffalo roamed in fair numbers. Hunting pressure had not yet driven the wapiti back into the high country which eventually became its home. Mule deer offered sport and a handy alternative source of meat. The presence of buffalo wolves and the two species of bear did nothing to detract from the pleasure of the trip and gave promise of additional hunting.

And there were pronghorn antelope.

Of all the animals Lord Henry saw, none attracted him as did these gaily colored, hock-horned, dainty creatures, which showed characteristics of the deer, antelope and goat families, yet belonged to none of them. From his first sight of the jet black horns, black and white face, tan and white ears, tan body striped with bars of white along the neck, and turning to white on its underside, and pure white rump, Lord Henry wanted to add one to his collection.

As Kerry warned, that did not prove easy. With its grass grazed down short by the enormous herds of buffalo, the rolling, open land of the Great Plains offered an ideal habitat for the pronghorn. Living in such country, possessed of a keen sense of smell, sharp hearing and probably the most far-sighted eyes of any animal, the pronghorn proved a worthy adversary in a battle of wits.

During the first two days' travel Lord Henry practiced with his Remington and could achieve accuracy at ranges of up to a quarter of a mile. Getting into even that distance proved to be anything but a sinecure. No matter how far a herd scattered while feeding, at least one of its members always seemed to spot the approaching hunter. Once seen, the pronghorn gave warning in a manner unique to its kind. The large white patch on the rump covered muscular discs which contracted when the animal was disturbed, causing the hairs to rise abruptly and reflect the sun's light. After one animal gave its warning flash, accompanied by a powerful aroma from scent glands along the discs, others saw and repeated it until every pronghorn in the area had been alerted. Any further alarm sent the entire herd speeding off, running at a pace the best horses in the remuda could not equal.

For ten days Lord Henry tried to take a pronghorn—not just any one, but the biggest and best buck available—and met with no success. Once, on the fifth day, he carried out a fine stalk and then made the mistake of peering cautiously over a rim to take a final survey of the situation. Although the nearer animals missed spotting him, a buck half a mile away saw his head and knew it had not been there when last studying the rim. Instantly the buck flashed its warning and the herd went racing off to safety. Twice, after abortive stalks, Lord Henry tried to shoot one of the escaping animals on the run, only to miscalculate their speed and see his lead strike well behind the big bucks which invariably brought up the rear.

Kerry and Lord Henry tried to improve the peer's accuracy on moving targets, spending a whole day with the hunter galloping by at varying ranges and dragging an empty kerosene can behind him on the end of a thirty-foot length of rope. While Lord Henry soon developed the knack of swinging the rifle, leading the can so that the bullet met it, he found doing the same on a speeding antelope far harder.

All the camp watched and waited, although Frank Mayer's crew and the old hound-dog man wondered why Lord Henry went to so much trouble when he might ambush a waterhole, or use a relay of horses to run a herd into exhaustion so as to make picking off one of its members easy. Such an idea was not acceptable to the peer's sense of sportsmanship and fair play. To make up in a small way for his disappointment with the pronghorn, Lord Henry took a very good, six-point mule deer after a careful stalk, and from a range of three hundred yards, the closest he could get without being detected. He also dropped a large dog buffalo wolf as it stood tearing flesh from a buffalo calf dragged down by the pack.

Before the first week ended the party had settled down into their routine. Each morning after breakfast Kerry and Lord Henry took their horses and Shaun to ride out in search of sport. Killem handled the breaking of the camp, following a predetermined route to the next stopping place. Depending on their luck, the hunters would join the rest of the party either on the trail or at the next camp.

Although it might be far different from the life she led in England, Beryl found little difficulty in settling down. Experience in India and Africa helped, and she had the very able hands of Calamity Jane to guide her in the business of living on the Great Plains. It became a convention that Beryl kept the camp supplied with meat. When available, Kerry took her out. If not, she went with old Sassfitz Kane, the hound-dog man, and never failed to return without bringing something suitable for the table. In addition to hunting, she overcame the cook's aversion to having women around his fire and learned much about his trade.

Wheatley took the new life in his stride. On the first night out, the wrangler—a brawny but far from bright young man—cast doubts about the valet's manhood. Requesting the insulting young man to walk into the bushes, Wheatley peeled off his jacket and demonstrated a knowledge of fist-fighting which left the other sprawled flat, dazed, sorry and much wiser. After that, Wheatley had no further trouble and became very popular with the other members of the camp staff.

"We'll be off the Plains soon, Henry," Kerry remarked as they rode far ahead of the party on the early afternoon of the eleventh day.

Already the ground tended to rise in higher folds and trees scattered here and there instead of rocks and bushes which had been the feature since leaving Otley Creek. Both men understood the full significance of Kerry's comment as they studied the changed scenery. The pronghorn lived in open country, not among the wooded land of the hills which drew nearer with each passing mile.

"It looks that way," the peer agreed.

"We could make camp for a few days to let you make a try at taking a pronghorn," the hunter suggested.

"I'll leave it to you, old chap. But I thought you wanted to get into the hill country."

"I do," agreed Kerry. "Out here on the Plains we can be seen for miles and Indians have been known to attack even when they're supposed to be at peace. Besides, the elk'll be starting their rut soon and that's the best time to get a real big buck."

"And we do have a long way to go yet," Lord Henry said, thoughtfully. "If we stay here even for a few days, we'll miss some of the other stuff I want."

"Sure. Only I'd sure like to see you get a pronghorn."

Almost as soon as he spoke, Kerry saw one of the antelope appear from a distant valley and halt to snip off leaves from a bitterbush. Instantly Kerry halted his gray and Lord Henry brought his mount to a stop. Without needing a word of command, Shaun dropped to the ground and lay still.

"What is it?" asked the peer.

"Over there," Kerry answered. "Almost in line with that biggest hill. Can you see him?"

"Only just," admitted Lord Henry and slowly eased the field glasses from his saddle-pouch.

Moving just as slowly and cautiously, the peer raised his glasses, focused them and studied the enlarged view of the pronghorn. Over the past few days he had studied many antelope and could tell the good from the average.

That buck browsing in the distance was more than good, being the finest specimen Lord Henry had yet seen. One sure way of estimating a pronghorn's trophy value was to study its head. If the horns' length appeared to equal that from tip of nose to base of skull, then it was a trophy well worth trying for. The buck that Lord Henry studied carried horns which looked even longer than the head. Nor were they narrow freak growths but massive, with well-developed prongs and a matching pair of rear-pointing tips.

"Do you want him?" Kerry asked.

"Do I want my right arm?" demanded the Englishman, showing more emotion than usual. "Where're the rest of his herd?"

Eagerly both men scanned the surrounding area, but could see no sign of other pronghorns.

"He's alone," Kerry finally stated.

"An old buck run off from the herd, like the buffalo," Lord Henry agreed. "That could make things easier, only having one pair of eyes to watch for."

"Don't sell him short on that score," warned Kerry. "He might be alone, but he's still as keen as ever. Maybe more so, having to depend on hisself. This's going to take some mighty smart figuring if you're going to get him."

"I could make a circle, come in through that broken country," Lord Henry said, studying the land with the eye of a tactician.

"There's no cover within five hundred yards of him," Kerry pointed out.

"Except for that tree," Lord Henry answered, even before Kerry could say it.

"Yeah. Happen you can keep that between you and him, you might be able to either walk or crawl up close. If you reach the tree, you'll only be around a hundred and fifty yards from him. It won't be easy."

"What would be the pleasure if it was?"

"Leave us try to even the odds just a mite," Kerry drawled. "I've found a lone buck'll not take to running unless he figures he's in danger. Happen he sees a man in the distance, he'll go on eating, but watch him and not run until the feller comes closer. Now if I edge into sight, he'll likely watch me and let you move in behind him."

"It's worth a try," Lord Henry said and slipped from his saddle. At the left of the saddle hung the Remington Creedmoor in a boot, the big eight-bore double riding on the right. Taking the single-shot, Lord Henry gave Kerry an excited grin and moved off.

As soon as the peer disappeared into cover, Kerry rode forward, leading the other horse. Three quarters of a mile away, the buck antelope's head jerked up and it stared in the hunter's direction. Immediately Kerry halted the horses and swung from the saddle. He sat down on the ground, Shaun flopping at his side, and saw to his relief that the buck behaved in the expected manner. After studying Kerry for a short time, it resumed feeding but continued to dart glances in his direction.

Slipping into the bottom of a draw, Lord Henry strode along it for a time. On reaching a point where it swung away from his desired direction, he climbed the side and peered very cautiously over. Everything appeared to be going according to plan. The pronghorn still browsed on the bitterbush, and in the distance Kerry sat by his gray like a statue, Shaun at his side.

Lord Henry crawled over the draw's rim and advanced to the next cover on his belly, the rifle resting across his arms. Moving from rocks to bushes in a fast run if possible, or crawling on his belly when necessary, Lord Henry managed to put the trunk of the tree between himself and the pronghorn. For a few seconds he paused, catching his breath, then walked forward. Not even when stalking a Cape buffalo or African elephant had the Englishman taken so much care or felt such anxiety. If he could reach the tree undetected, he would be within a hundred and fifty yards of the buck, a mere spitting distance for such an accurate rifle as the Remington.

Sweat ran down the peer's face and he raised his left hand to wipe it from his eyes. Each foot tested the ground before taking the weight of his body on it. He reached fifty yards distance from the tree and wished he could see what the prong-horn did, but it stood hidden by the tree trunk. However, Kerry remained immobile on the rim, so all must still be well.

At that moment the pronghorn came into view. Having finished its browsing, it moved around the bush in search of shade. Only for an instant did it stand and stare at the man, then whirled and raced away. Bounding forward, Lord Henry tried to reach a position from where he could take a shot. He dropped to one knee at the bounding white ball which the buck's rump resembled, but he did not fire at such a poor target when to do so might result in nothing more than a wounded, lost animal, doomed to a lingering death.

Up on the distant rim Kerry cursed the luck and moved his gray forward. Shaun came to his feet with a lithe bound, but at that instant not even a sight-hunting dog like the wolfhound could see a moving object. However, the pronghorn could see and made out a wolf-like shape alongside the man and horse. Whirling around in a tight turn, the buck raced off in the opposite direction and on a course which carried it across Lord Henry's front at a range of two hundred yards. The antelope's speed made it so difficult a target, for it ran smoothly and in a manner far different from the bounding, leaping gait of a fleeing whitetail or mule deer. Lord Henry sighted carefully and swung his rifle ahead almost two and a half times the speeding buck's length. Still swinging, he squeezed the trigger. Flame erupted from the Remington's barrel and smoke momentarily hid the buck from Lord Henry's sight. Although the recoil of the heavy rifle was not small, the peer felt nothing of it.

Bullet and pronghorn sped along their converging courses, the first invisible in its speed, the second almost so. Vaguely through the dispersing smoke, Lord Henry saw the pronghorn bound into the air and, when it landed, go crashing to the ground.

Leaping to his feet, Lord Henry forgot his habitual calm, or even to take the basic precaution of reloading his single-shot rifle. He let out a yell of delight and raced forward. On the rim, Kerry sent the horses galloping in the direction of the antelope, waving his new Stetson over his head and whooping his pleasure. Even Shaun appeared to catch the excitement and wagged his tail on approaching Lord Henry.

"That was as good a shot as I've ever seen," Kerry said, almost reverently, as they stood side by side and looked down at the pronghorn. "I thought we'd lost him when he started to run."

"So did I," admitted Lord Henry. "It put years on me."

"Two hundred yards at least and with the buck on the run," enthused Kerry. "That's shooting."

"It'll be three hundred yards by the time the wagon gets here," grinned the peer. "And before the trip's over I'll be dropping him at four hundred. I wouldn't be at all surprised if I bagged the little blighter at half a mile at least by the time I reach London again."

"Yeah, these things grow," Kerry answered understandingly.

A low warning growl from Shaun chopped off Kerry's comments on the way in which the distance at which a trophy was taken increased. Even before he turned, the hunter could guess what he would see—and hoped he might be wrong. Only one creature in the United States could cause that hair-bristling, scared attitude which Shaun showed as he stood on stiff legs and glared behind the men.

So interested in the trophy had the men been that only Shaun's warning saved them, or gave them a chance of survival, for two hunters could hardly have found themselves in a more tricky and dangerous position.

Attracted by the wind-carried scent of the pronghorn's blood, a hungry bear emerged from a draw not fifty yards away. Having been denned up down-wind, it avoided detection by Shaun until it came into sight and headed toward the scent which attracted its attention. It was not a black bear, comparatively mild and timid, but a large grizzly and as such reigned as king of the Great Plains. Seeing two men and the dog did not swerve the bear from its purpose. Hunger pangs gnawed at it, the scent of blood told it that food lay close at hand, and it did not intend allowing such a small consideration as the presence of other creatures to stand in its way.

"Watch it, Henry!" Kerry yelled. "Grizzly!"

The big hunter knew their danger, conscious of the fact that his carbine, an inadequate weapon under the circumstances—hung in the saddleboot on his gray. At the same moment Lord Henry became aware that he held an empty rifle. To one side, the horses screamed in fear and tried to tear their reins free from the bush to which the big hunter tied them on arrival. Before either man could move, Kerry saw his gray drag free and race away. Then both he and Lord Henry hurled themselves toward the peer's mount.

While Shaun charged at the bear, he had more sense than to tangle head on with seven hundred or so pounds of Great Plain grizzly. Swerving aside, the wolfhound avoided the bear's rush and went for it as it passed. Not even Shaun's large and powerful jaws could penetrate deep enough through the grizzly's long, thick coat to do any damage, but the attack slowed and distracted the bear for a few vital seconds. Although unable to reach flesh, Shaun clung on to the mouthful of hair.

Lord Henry reached the horse first, its pitching and fighting prevented him from sliding the Evans big bore out of the boot. Just as he had the rifle halfway out, the horse crashed into him and knocked him staggering. The bear swung in Lord Henry's direction, ignoring and barely slowed by Shaun's weight dragging on his flank.

Jerking out his axe, Kerry slashed the leather of the saddle-boot and his other hand tore free the rifle. Letting the axe fall, he threw the Evans to his shoulder as he whirled around. The gun rose just as smoothly as when he tried it in the room at the Otley Creek Hotel, its hammers gliding back easily under his thumb and the twin tubes aiming in the required direction almost without conscious effort on his part.

With a strange rifle in his hands, Kerry did not dare go for the deadly and immediate-resulting neck shot. If he missed the comparatively narrow vertebrae, all he would achieve was enraging the animal even more. Nor did time permit him to make a lung shot which would kill eventually. Instead, he aimed at an angle that would drive the lead into the bear's thick coat and break one, if not both, shoulders. If he could do that, the grizzly would go down.

Squeezing the trigger for the right barrel, Kerry learned what it felt like to use the big double. The Evans roared, its recoil slamming Kerry back on to his heels and tilting the barrels high into the air. If a second shot had been needed, Kerry could never have brought the gun down into line fast enough to fire it.

Caught in the shoulder by the shattering impact of the heavy bullet, the grizzly was knocked staggering. That rifle had been designed to halt a charging elephant, Cape buffalo or rhinoceros in its tracks and, formidable though it might be, the grizzly could not be compared with any of them in size or bulk. If Kerry had been using a less powerful rifle, even his Sharps Old Reliable, Lord Henry might have been badly mauled. Catching his foot on something, already off balance and reeling from the horse's shove, the peer went sprawling on the ground just ahead of the bear. He saw his danger and rolled hurriedly aside, but the bullet deflected the bear so that, when it fell, it missed his body by inches. For all that, Lord Henry continued rolling until safely clear of the snarling, thrashing animal.

"Grab the hoss!" Kerry yelled.

Rising hurriedly, Lord Henry dived for and grabbed the horse's reins just as they parted company with the bush. He went hand over hand up to the head-stall, caught hold of it and drew down the horse's head. Retaining his hold, he used his hands and voice to restrain and calm the frightened animal. With that vitally important task completed, he looked in Kerry's direction.

"Finish him off, old chap," Lord Henry said, nodding to the struggling bear. "He's your bird."

"Now me, I'd say he was more bear than bird," Kerry replied. "Toss me a bullet for your Remington and I'll slop him."

"I only heard you fire the Evans once," Lord Henry pointed out, reaching into his jacket pocket.

"And that's all you're likely to hear me fire it," stated Kerry. "Any time I want a bust shoulder, I'll lie down and let Calam run her wagon over it."

"As you wish, old chap," grinned Lord Henry. "And thanks."

Watching Kerry load the Remington, Lord Henry decided that today was a day on the Great Plains he would never forget. Kerry took aim with the Remington and drove a bullet into the grizzly's head. After the impact of the Evans eight-bore, the kick of the ninety-grain powder charge used by the .44 'Special' caliber Creedmore seemed barely noticeable.

"No sign of your horse, old chap," Lord Henry said. "He took off fast."

"Likely still running," Kerry replied. "We'll load up the pronghorn and make for the wagons. With any luck, he'll find his way to them."

Chapter 12

A BUNCH OF UNWELCOME VISITORS

~

"NOW YOU STOP YOUR WORRYING, GAL," CALAMITY told Lady Beryl as the blonde stood by the end of her wagon and looked off through the gathering darkness. "They'll be along soon enough."

"I suppose so," Beryl replied. "I'm not really worried, Kerry knows what he's doing."

"I'd say old Hank does too," grinned Calamity. "Or if they don't by now, I reckon they never will."

"It's just that Ker—they've never stayed away this late before."

"There're a whole heap of reasons for that," Calamity pointed out. "I know hunting men.

There ain't the one of them who remembers time or anything when he's out hunting."

Having seen no sign of Kerry and Lord Henry since breaking camp that morning, the remainder of the party continued their journey and made camp by a small lake. They halted earlier than usual, the lake offering the best camping ground available in the area. While the men set up tents and attended to their chores, Calamity and Beryl had been hunting for camp meat and the girl shot a prime bull elk which necessitated the services of Wheatley, Sassfitz Kane and the skinner loaned by Frank Mayer to butcher and collect. Neither the butchering party nor the two male hunters had returned as the sun began to sink in the west and Beryl spent enough time standing by Calamity's wagon staring off into the distance, that the other girl joined her with a word of advice.

"Then stop tearing lumps out of that fancy lady's nose-rag," Calamity said.

"I'm not te——" began Beryl, then looked at the crumpled wisp of cloth clenched in her hand. "Why you——"

"Yeah, I know I am," admitted Calamity. "It's— who's this coming?"

Muffled by the springy, close-cropped grass, even a large party of horsemen did not make too much noise as long as they held their horses to a walk. Eight men approached the camp, three of them leading loaded pack mules and one with a saddled, riderless horse fastened to his mount's rig.

"That horse!" Beryl gasped. "It's Kerry's gray."

"Damned if it's not," Calamity replied and shot out a hand to catch the other girl's arm as Beryl started to move forward. "Hold hard there."

"But it's *his* horse!" Beryl gasped.

"There're a whole heap of good reasons why they've got it," Calamity replied. "Might be they found it straying and brought it here to ask if we know who owns it."

"But what——"

"A good way to find out'd be wait and see."

"I—I suppose you're right," Beryl said, making an effort and regaining her usual composure.

While Beryl accepted Calamity's judgment, the red-head felt just a mite uneasy as she studied the approaching party with range-wise eyes. Unless Calamity missed her guess, that bunch would be highly unlikely to return any horse they found straying to its owner, or try to locate the owner. All the group appeared to be well armed, rode good horses, yet did not have the appearance of ordinary Great Plains travellers. Their clothing, a hybrid mixture of town and range styles, did not point to their working at any of the normal Great Plains professions. Caution and sullen-eyed truculence showed in their attitudes, and most of them carried rifles on their saddles.

Standing alongside the fire, Doc Killem threw a glance at the cook and then turned his gaze back to the approaching men. His conclusions followed the same line as Calamity's and his eyes narrowed on coming to the gray. At that moment Killem realized just how few of his party remained in the camp. Three men butchering Beryl's elk, the wrangler holding the remuda down by the edge of the lake; Kerry and Lord Henry away hunting, that left only the cook and the big freighter on hand. Not good odds when he took note of the newcomers' behavior.

Range etiquette required that a party approaching another's camp halted at a distance and went through the formality of calling for permission to enter. Unless some emergency called for it, the newcomers should never come into a camp area with drawn weapons on their saddles. The eight men failed to observe either rule as they rode in.

"You got coffee going?" demanded the big, scar-faced man who appeared to be heading the party and who had Kerry's gray fastened to his saddle-horn.

"Sure," Killem answered coldly.

"Food too?"

A low snort from the cook showed his opinion

of the newcomers' behavior. He gave the stew in the pot over the fire a stir and threw a glance to where his ten-gauge shotgun rested in a handy position, but waited for Killem to make the play before trying to reach the weapon.

"We've food on," Killem agreed.

The scar faced man threw a quick look around the camp area, taking in the two men and leering toward the women. Behind him, the others shot calculating glances about them. To the watching Calamity, their actions reminded her of a pack of wolves sizing up a deer herd for an attack. However, like the cook, she awaited Killem's lead before taking cards.

"Reckon me 'n' the boys'll take us a bite then," announced Scar-Face.

"Just like that, huh?" Killem grunted.

"Just like that—all eight of us."

"I've counted you."

"You want maybe paying for the food?" sneered Scar-Face, his accent eastern even though he affected western clothes.

Cold anger glowed in Killem's eyes at the words. A James Black bowie-knife hung at his left side and an 1860 Army Colt rode in a fast-draw holster at his right. He could use either weapon with some skill, but knew that he had not the necessary speed to draw and throw down on the men before one or more got a rifle working. What Killem needed right then was a diversion, something to take the men's attention from him for a vital instant.

"You could try paying by telling me where you got the gray," Killem answered, as he watched Calamity walking in a significant direction.

"There's some'd call that question real nosey," purred Scar-Face.

Behind the leader, one of the bunch let his hand fall to the butt of his holstered revolver and felt sure that neither of the men by the fire could see him making the move. Nor could they, but Calamity stood in a more advantageous position and had the means to prevent such an action.

Slipping free her whip, she snaked its lash behind her and gauged the distance with her eye. Too far to reach the man, or his horse, and no time to get closer; even if she could do so without drawing attention to herself. However, the man, on the flank of the party, led a pack mule and the animal stood closer than he did to Calamity's position.

Forward flickered the whip, its tip catching the mule on the rump in a manner liable to sting through the animal's thick hide. Few creatures in the world were capable of showing their objections more thoroughly or spectacularly than a mule. On feeling the sting of the lash, the animal gave out a squeal of rage and bounded into the air, twisting its body in a manner that crashed its pack into the horse which led it. The horse's rider, taken completely by surprise, yelled, pitched out of his saddle, and forgot all about drawing his revolver

Instantly one of the other mules joined in the fuss and some confusion disrupted the ranks of the newcomers. Nor did the explosive pop of Calamity's big whip, drawn back and shot out again, lessen the desired effect. Given his diversion, Killem slid out his Army Colt and the cook discarded his spoon, replacing it by the shotgun, which he lined on the men.

One of the men bounded from his horse, landed spraddle-legged and reached for his Colt. Being partially hidden from his companion, he failed to take Calamity into account. By that time Calamity had advanced to more accurate range and her whip coiled out once again, wrapping around the man's right ankle and heaving on it. With a yell the man tipped sideways as his foot left the ground. Shaking free her whip's lash in a smooth move, Calamity gave warning to her first victim as he came to his knees, spluttering curses and reaching for his revolver once more.

"Try it and I'll chop your hand off!" she snapped.

At the same moment she felt her Navy Colt slide from its holster. "You don't need it, Calam," said Beryl's voice.

Having seen the blonde shoot a handgun, Calamity raised no objections. Beryl might not have Mark Counter's ability or knowledge of gunfighting, but could hit her target with enough accuracy to make her an asset in the game.

"Let's have no more moves, gents!" Killem ordered, his Colt being more than adequately backed by the yawning barrels of the cook's pacifier.

"There'd best not be," agreed the cook, glancing quickly at his pot. "If that stew burns, somebody'll wish his maw and pappy never met the one time they did."

Charging up, a Springfield Army carbine in his hands, the wrangler added his quota to the camp's defense-force, which received further reinforcements in the shape of Wheatley and Sassfitz Kane, who had been riding in unobserved when Calamity stirred up the pot and brought it to a boil.

Faced with so much opposition and thrown into confusion, the newcomers forgot any objections they might have felt to Killem questioning them and put aside whatever plans they might have made.

"We'll have all them rifles on the ground and you bunch stood in line so I can see you all," Killem went on, after the newcomers managed to quieten down their mounts and pack animals.

"Hell, this's fine hospitality," Scar-Face answered sullenly. "We ride in here looking for a meal——"

A ringing whoop from the west broke through and ended the man's words. Only Beryl of the party turned her head from the visitors and looked to where her brother walked alongside Kerry, leading a well-loaded horse from out of the west.

"There's a feller coming up now who's going to be mighty interested in hearing how you came by that gray," Killem warned.

"And he's got a real persuasive way with him for getting answers, too," the cook continued, laying aside his shotgun and giving the stew a stir.

"Hell, we found it straying and brought it along," answered Scar-Face.

"Yeah," said Killem dryly. "We saw how eager you was to ask if it belonged to any of us."

"I figured you'd ask about the hoss if it did. And if we'd asked you, what'd stop you claiming it was yours whether you owned it or not?"

On the face of it, the man could have been telling the truth. A fine animal like the gray was worth money, even without its saddle and the Winchester carbine. So Scar-Face could be exercising caution and trying to avoid allowing the horse to fall into the wrong hands. Only he and his party did not strike Killem as the kind who would bother unduly about such minor points.

"Ain't heard nor seen a thing to say that feller who's coming owns it, anyways," a bearded man growled.

"Happen you aim to call him a liar, or take up the point, do it gentle, mister," drawled the cook. "That's Kerry Barran's hoss and he thinks high of it."

Clearly Kerry's name meant something to at least half of the surly bunch. One of its members, a slender, sallow-faced and untidy young man wearing a dirty town suit, showed some concern at hearing the identity of the approaching owner of the gray.

Calamity sensed Beryl's agitation and found it distracting at a time when she felt all her attention should be kept on the business at hand.

"For Tophet's sake!" she hissed. "Go meet him and tell him he's been worrying you sick."

Throwing an annoyed look at the red-head, Beryl snorted, "It's only natural that I should be worried about my *brother*."

"Oh sure," agreed the unabashed Calamity. "And I just bet you never gave Kerry a single thought at all."

Fortunately the light had gone sufficiently to prevent Beryl's blush showing. For the first time she appeared to have lost her composure, but regained it quickly. Calamity meant nothing by her comments and, after all, Beryl did regard Kerry with considerably more interest than one might expect between employer and a hired man.

"I have been a little worried about Kerry, too," she admitted.

"Then you go tell him," Calamity suggested. "We can handle this bunch. It'd be best if you told Kerry and Hank what's happening."

Although Beryl ran to meet the approaching men, she could not force herself to show Kerry her real feelings for him. Nor, if it came to a point, had the big hunter ever given a hint that he might regard her as more than a friendly employer who was willing to lend a sympathetic ear to his dreams for the future. Not wishing to offend the hunter by appearing to throw herself at him, even if her upbringing allowed her to do such a thing, Beryl avoided making what might look like the first move to a closer understanding.

"Is there some fuss down there, Beryl?" Kerry asked, holding Henry's Remington in his right hand.

"Not now. A bunch of toughs came into camp leading your horse and tried to cut up rough when we asked about it. Calamity, Dobe and Cookie handled them."

"We saw something of it, old thing," Lord Henry put in. "Any idea who they might be?"

"None at all. Those chaps just arrived without as much as a 'by-your-leave' and started demanding food and coffee. I—we—we were rather worried when we saw your horse, Kerry. Then when the men turned ugly, I—we thought something had happened to you."

"It nearly did," Lord Henry said. "Had a little trouble with a grizzly."

At which point Beryl saw the pronghorn's body draped across the saddle and the rolled-up bear's hide lashed behind it.

"I see you got your antelope," she said. "Is it a good one, dear?"

"Eighteen inches over the curves," Lord Henry declared, proudly, meaning the length of the horns. "I bagged it on the run at three hun—over two hundred yards."

The correction came as the peer caught Kerry's grinning face and accusing eye. However, by that time they had come close enough to the camp for Kerry to take a good look at the newcomers. What he saw and remembered about that bunch wiped the smile from his face. Beryl could see the uneasiness showed by the eight men as Kerry approached them.

"Hello, Jenkins," the big hunter greeted.

"We found your hoss straying, Barran," the scar-faced man answered hurriedly. "Brought it here and this lot jumped us afore we could say a word."

"I just bet they did," drawled Kerry, his eyes running along the line of men until they reached the lean, sallow-faced one. "Looks like there're a lot of old friends here, doesn't it, Shaun?"

With that Kerry took a step in the sallow young man's direction, Shaun bristling dangerously at his side. Fear came to the young man's face and he made a hurried pace to the rear as if to hide behind his companions. Showing real loyalty, the men he tried to use as cover kept out of the path of the advancing hunter.

"No!" screeched the sallow young man. "It wasn't me. I didn't— —"

"I know what you did and lying won't help you," Kerry interrupted. "Now I ought to let you see what the coon got because of you."

"I didn't send him after you!" the man yelled, terror on his face. "Keep that dog off of me."

For a moment Kerry stood indecisive. One word from him would send Shaun springing forward to tear the man's throat out; and, the way Kerry saw it, the other deserved that fate. Kerry had sworn to take revenge on the man when next they met, but with the opportunity at hand, he could not force himself to give the order to the waiting dog.

"I'm trying to break Shaun of jumping skunk, so

you're safe," Kerry finally growled. "Now get the hell far away from me, and do it fast."

Turning, the young man went at a staggering run to where his horse waited. None of the others needed further urging but followed on his heels. Kerry stood with the Remington gripped in his hands. Shaun sat at his side, neither taking their eyes from the departing bunch until they passed out of sight.

"We'd best double the guard tonight, Dobe," the hunter declared as he turned to his companions.

"I reckon you could be right," Killem answered. "You know them from some place, Kerry?"

"I know 'em."

"Do you think they'll be back?" asked Lord Henry.

"I don't reckon so," Kerry answered. "But I'd sooner not count on it."

While the others gathered to help unload and examine the trophies of the day's hunt, Kerry returned to his gray. As he looked the horse over, Beryl walked across and stood by him.

"Where did you know them from, Kerry?" she asked.

"Back on the railroad. Some of them anyway."

"Did they work for it?"

"You might call it that. Most of the time the big

jasper with the scar and the thin young cuss tried to stir up trouble among the gandy dancers.

"Gandy dancers?"

"Construction hands. Varley, the thin one, was the leader. He's educated, a thinker—though I'd sooner not have his thoughts. Jenkins was the muscle. From the start they were trouble. You know the thing, equality for everybody."

"Only they mean bringing everybody down to the level of the lowest," Beryl agreed. "We have some of them in England."

"You've got them. Hating the guts of anybody who had more than them and looking down on the men they were supposed to help. Just using them to get what they themselves wanted."

"You didn't like them?"

"They didn't go for me," Kerry corrected. "I figure if a man's paying me, I owe him a good day's work, which didn't set right with them. Food wasn't too good at first and they'd almost brought work to a stop, stirring up the men with talk about the employers not keeping promises. So when I started hunting and bringing in fresh meat, it didn't set too well with Varley or any of his bunch. I gave Jenkins that scar when he tried to jump me."

"And the other one, the thin chap?" asked Beryl. "Did he try to do anything against you?"

"Not him," Kerry growled. "He's the kind who always gets somebody else to do the dirty work."

"Who did he get?"

"There was a coon Varley had around all the time. Well, Varley got him all liquored up one night and stirred him up against Southerners on the old slavery hates. Then sent him after me. The coon came with a razor and Shaun jumped him, killed him before I could do a thing."

"What happened then?"

"I went after Varley, but he ran out. The company fired the rest of the bunch next morning and ran them off. I knew there'd be trouble if I stayed on, too. The other coons wouldn't give a thought to why that feller died, that he'd been drinking and sent to kill me, and they'd be after me. Varley had them all boiling with hate against the whites so that they figured one of their own kind couldn't do a thing wrong. The damnable part is that, until Varley started stirring them up, the checkerboard crews got on fine. By the time he'd done, they had to make up white and black gangs and keep them well apart. Nobody had thought of skin color until he got among them, but they did after Shaun killed the coon. The blacks wanted my hide and the whites sided me. Rather than be the cause of bad fuss, I pulled out."

"So Varley cost you your job?" Beryl said.

"In a way," Kerry answered. "I'd been thinking of pulling out for some time. I'd grown tired of shooting a buffalo for its tongue and maybe some of the hump, leaving the rest to rot. I pulled out and tried homesteading, but got wiped out. Then I wound up doing something even more distasteful than meat-hunting."

"That's all behind you now," Beryl told him.

"I reckon it is. Well, I'd best take the horses to the remuda."

"I'll come along with you for the walk."

After helping Kerry and the wrangler to tend to the horses, Beryl did not rush back to the camp. For the first time she and the hunter went beyond the casual friendship of the past days. On returning to the camp, they could hear Lord Henry talking.

"And I finally bagged him on the run at at least three hundred yards."

Chapter 13

A RIDERLESS HORSE MEANS TROUBLE

"THERE'S A CHANGE IN THE PACK'S VOICE NOW," Lord Henry commented, as he halted his horse and looked across the ridged hill country.

"They've got that old painter up a tree," Sassfitz Kane replied, cocking his head to one side and listening to the steady coarse chop of the hounds baying. Mingled with it came the deeper bark of the wolfhound and the old-timer went on, "I see that old Shaun dog's right there with them, Kerry."

"Sounds that way," agreed the hunter. "Best get to them."

"You in a rush to get back and see somebody?" grinned Kane.

A slight flush of red tinged Kerry's tanned face. "You know the gals are off hunting together, and I don't like for them to be on their own after meeting Varley's bunch."

"Sure," Kane replied amiably. "We've been falling over their sign every day for the past week."

During the seven days since the hectic meeting with the ex railroad trouble-makers, Kerry's party had seen no more sign of the others' presence. Kerry took their trail at dawn the next day and found them to be moving steadily away toward the hills. As a precaution, he led his own party at an angle away from the line taken by Varley's bunch, and after the third night went back to normal instead of subjecting everybody to double guard duty.

Since the night of Varley's visit, relations between Beryl and Kerry had changed. At first it had not been noticeable, but the blonde and the hunter drew closer together and spent as much time as they could in each other's company. Every day after the hunting ended, Kerry either took Beryl riding or went walking with her. Calamity heartily approved of the situation, but could not help wondering how Lord Henry regarded it. Being a forthright young lady, she decided to take up the matter at the first opportunity. So far it had not come and she, forthright or not, realized tact would be needed if she wanted to avoid doing more harm than good.

Once in the hills, hunting absorbed everybody's attention. Lord Henry took a cock turkey, a good bull elk, and added a black bear to his growing collection of trophies. The Wind River country, as Kerry promised, produced well and the party moved deeper along the river's course, looking for a place to halt for an extended stay.

While hunting ahead, Kerry and Lord Henry had found the freshly killed body of a deer. From the fact that the deer was killed by being bitten below the base of the skull, and other signs, Kerry concluded a cougar brought it down. Deciding to take the chance and add a cougar to the collection, they returned to the main body with the intention of bringing Beryl along to see the hounds work. Beryl and Calamity, the latter declaring she needed a rest from team driving, had already left the others to hunt for camp meat, and so looked like missing the first opportunity to see Kane's hounds in action.

Knowing his sister's keenness at following the hounds, she rode to hunt regularly while in England, Lord Henry could guess at her disappointment when she heard what she had missed, but if they delayed while somebody went out to locate the girls, he might lose the cougar. So he decided to go out, knowing there would be other chances for his sister to follow the hounds before the trip ended.

Already the chase had lasted for three miles, with plenty of hard riding and excitement. Once the cougar stopped to make a fight, holding off the pack even though Shaun ran with it. That fact led Kerry and Kane to suspect that they hunted a large, powerful tom in the prime of life; one worthy of being called a trophy.

At one point the cougar crossed a valley down which the horses could not go. By the time the hunters found a place where they could ascend and then climbed up to the other side, the chase had drawn far ahead and only the baying of the four hound-dogs guided them.

Following the sound of the hounds baying "treed," Kerry and the other two men left the valley rim and rode on. Half a mile passed and they saw the dogs at the foot of a huge tree, scrabbling or rearing against its trunk, staring up to where a large tom cougar lay snarling defiance down at them from a limb.

"There's your cougar, Henry," Kerry drawled. "Get down and take him."

Unshipping his Express rifle, Lord Henry swung from his saddle. "I'd rather get in closer so there's no chance of wounding him."

"You'd best not wound him," warned Kane soberly. "Happen he lands among the hounds alive, he'll cut some of them to ribbons."

"I'll make sure of him, or not shoot," promised the peer.

"If he runs again, there's a cliff wall about a quarter of a mile on," Kerry said. "He can get up it, but neither hoss nor hound can. This's your chance of taking him, maybe the only one you'll get."

"Leave it to me," smiled Lord Henry.

Walking forward, the peer saw the cougar turn its head in his direction and its devil's mask face twisted in a snarl which showed long canine fangs. As if sensing the man offered a greater menace than did the dogs, the cougar crouched. Sleek muscles rippled under its tawny coat and it launched itself from the branch in one of the long, fluid leaps for which the mountain lion had long been famous. Clear over the heads of the hounds sailed the cougar, making for the thick bushes beyond where it had been forced to climb into the tree.

Lord Henry threw up the Express, its butt nestling into his shoulder and his right eye aligning the sights. Smoothly he swung, like following a rising pheasant with a shotgun, then touched off his shot. A scream burst from the cougar's lips and its body arched under the impact of the bullet. From a smoothly curving bound, its flight became a plummet to the ground. Even as the cougar crashed down on its side, the pack charged forward.

"Git back, blast ye!" bellowed Kane, advancing hurriedly. "Call that overgrowed critter of your'n away so's I can deal with mine, Kerry."

"He's dead, old chap, so he can't harm them," objected Lord Henry.

"Naw. But they'll make a hell of a mess of his hide happen we don't stop 'em," Kane replied.

Running forward, Kerry grabbed Shaun by the scruff of the neck and hauled the big dog away from the cougar's body. Once that danger had been removed, Kane drove off his hounds, preventing them from mauling and ruining the hide. Lord Henry stood back, a grin on his face as he listened to some of the choicer expressions Kane used to bring his dogs to order.

"You've quite a command of English," he commented.

"I've never yet seen a hound-dog who hadn't," Kerry remarked. "Reckon you can find your own way back to the wagons, Sassfitz?"

"If I can't, I deserve to get lost," replied the old man. "You still worrying about that lil gal?"

"Well, Kerry," said Lord Henry as they rode

away from where Kane started to skin the cougar. "Are you still worrying about Beryl?"

"You might say that," admitted Kerry.

"You're seeing rather a lot of her, aren't you?"

"It'd be hard not to, living like we do," Kerry answered, realizing that the expected subject had come up and wondering what the result would be.

"I mean rather more than just in the course of your professional duties."

"Yeah. I reckon I am."

"And your intentions?"

"Strictly honorable," Kerry spat out.

"My dear chap," Lord Henry drawled. "If I'd doubted *that* for a moment, I'd have cancelled the trip at the first hint."

"What would you say if I told you I aim to ask her to marry me?"

"I'd say the best of luck to you."

"You wouldn't try to stop her?" asked Kerry.

"Why should I try to influence her one way or the other?" Lord Henry said. "She's over twenty-one, and ought to be intelligent enough to know love from infatuation. In fact, I know she is."

"I can't offer anything like she's been used to," Kerry warned.

"Does Beryl know that?"

"It was the first thing I told her."

"And she said it didn't worry her in the least."

"How'd you know that?" asked Kerry, for Lord Henry made a statement instead of using the words as a question.

"She *is* my sister," Lord Henry reminded him. "I know how she thinks. Have you popped the question yet?"

"Not in so many words. I figured it was for me to ask you if I could first."

"Ask her, old son, by all means."

"I've no title——"

"It's surprising how few people have in the United States," replied Lord Henry. "You'll be making me think you're looking for a way out of it soon."

"I'm just telling——"

"I know what you're doing, and why, old chap," Lord Henry interrupted with a warm smile. "And I admire you for it. Don't let the title stand in your way. It's Beryl's happiness that counts. I'd rather see her marry you and be happy than force her into it with somebody the family might regard as more socially acceptable and spoil her—and his—life."

Relief flooded through Kerry at the words. One of the things he feared when thinking of Beryl had been how Lord Henry might take the news. Now he saw that he need have no worries on that score.

"Then I can go ahead and ask her?" he said.

"Don't let me stop you," smiled Lord Henry. "What're you planning to do if, or rather when, she accepts?"

"I've got some money saved. Not much, but enough for us to get started with a little horse ranch. We're going to stock it with wild stuff and try to improve the strain."

"That's a good idea. You both know horses. Beryl can handle her share of it. There'll be her marriage settlement, too. Dowry, you know."

"I'm not marrying her for that," Kerry snorted.

"I know you're not, old son. But it's part of the family tradition, and I'm insisting that you accept."

The discussion ended abruptly as Kerry pointed ahead of them to where smoke rose into the air. Not a single column such as a camp fire might make, or a dense cloud which might herald burning wagons, but a series of puffs that rose at regular intervals.

"That's for us!" he said. "Let's go."

Among other details arranged during the journey had been a signal to recall the hunters should their presence be urgently required at the camp. Kerry and Lord Henry exchanged glances, knowing what the smoke puffs meant, although not able to guess the nature of the emergency which demanded their recall. Without a word, they started their horses moving at a fast pace in the direction of the smoke puffs. Showing no signs of exhaustion after his long-chase, Shaun loped along by his master's side.

No hint of what might be wrong showed at the camp. A party of blue-clad U.S. Cavalry soldiers gathered by the fire, being fed by the cook, but they would not be sufficient reason for Killem to send up a smoke signal; unless they brought important news. Seeing the two riders, Dobe Killem walked from the fire. A tall, slim, young lieutenant followed on the big freighter's heels, his uniform well cut but travel-stained. Kerry and Lord Henry were less interested in the soldier than in the expression on the big freighter's normally emotionless face.

"We've got trouble," Killem told the men as they dismounted. "Lieutenant Dalby here brought Beryl's horse in."

"We found it straying, the reins fastened to its saddle," Dalby continued. "So my scout backtracked it. Found where it had been turned loose and were just about to investigate when your wagons came into sight. We came straight over to ask if the horse belonged here."

A riderless horse always caused concern in the West, where being mounted meant the difference between life and death, so the soldiers' actions did not surprise Kerry. In fact, he barely gave a thought to that aspect, being more concerned with how the horse came to be riderless in the first place. The horn-tied reins told him that all had not been well when the horse lost its rider. Like most people on the Great Plains, Beryl had her reins in two separate strands instead of being joined together. This was a precaution against being left afoot, for if something caused the rider to drop the reins, their trailing ends caught under the animal's feet and tended to prevent it running. Beryl knew better than to fasten the reins to the saddle-horn unless she did it deliberately to allow it free movement.

"What happened?" he growled.

"We followed the horse to where the ladies had shot a deer," Dalby explained. "They'd been standing by it when a bunch of men jumped them——"

"Indians?" asked Lord Henry.

"Not according to the scout," Dalby replied. "According to him, the men rode shod horses and wore boots. The way he read it, there'd been a scuffle either just before, or after, the horse got free. Then the ladies mounted on one horse and the whole bunch rode off."

"Let's get going, Henry," Kerry said quietly.

"Let's learn everything we can first," the peer answered. "We'll want fresh horses, Dobe, and——"

"I've got them waiting," Killem said. "Food's ready and waiting."

"Damn it, there's not time for food, with Beryl in danger!" Kerry roared.

"Calamity's in danger, too," Lord Henry pointed out. "But rushing off with empty bellies and on leg-weary horses won't get us to them any quicker."

Kerry's protests died away unsaid, for he knew Lord Henry spoke the truth. There was no way of knowing how long they might be on the trail, or what lay at the end of it. Fresh horses, a meal, spare food would prepare them the better for what lay ahead.

"I'll get the horses saddled," Killem told the hunters. "What rifles do you want along?"

"I'll take the Remington and the Winchester," answered Lord Henry. "How about you, Kerry?"

"Get my Sharps and the bullet box from the wagon, Dobe," Kerry said. "I've got the carbine, too. That should do me."

"All the crew reckon they're coming," Killem commented, before going to obey his orders.

"We may need them," Lord Henry replied, and headed for the fire. "Mr. Dalby, will you join us?"

"Thank you, sir," Dalby answered.

"How many men did your scout reckon them to be?" Kerry inquired. "Where is he? I don't see him around."

"Did he go alone?" Lord Henry asked.

"Sure. Figured it would be the best way. I know all he saw, though."

"Tell us about it, mister," ordered the peer, taking the plate of food from the cook.

"There seemed to be about half a dozen of them," said Dalby. "But—look there, it's my scout!"

Coming up at a gallop, a tall, buckskin-clad scout dropped from his lathered horse. "Lost 'em, mister," he said. "They took to some rocky ground that wouldn't hold tracks. But afore they did, they'd met up with another bunch. I reckon it's that crowd we've been hearing about."

"What crowd's that?" Kerry asked.

"There's a rumor of a bunch of bad whites holing up this way," explained Dalby. "Deserters from the Army, outlaws, riff-raff run out of the construction camps, that kind. Not that anybody's seen them, but there's been talk. A couple of immigrant families have disappeared going through this way. One of our patrols came on a burned-out wagon, but couldn't find any sign of who did it. I believe that Indians were responsible."

"You could be wrong, mister," Kerry growled. "Only a week back we saw a bunch who just about fitted your description. Run them out of our camp. If Beryl's in their hands——"

"How many men are supposed to be in this band?" Lord Henry asked.

"It's only rumor, but that says about thirty or more," the officer replied.

"Big odds for us," the peer commented. "Especially if they reach their main camp." His eyes went to the soldiers, then swung back to Dalby. "Your troop could be of assistance, Mr. Dalby."

"Yes, sir," agreed the officer, doubtfully.

Taking the President's letter from his pocket, Lord Henry held it toward Dalby. "This will indemnify you against disobeying any orders you may have."

On reading the President's instructions, Lieutenant Dalby showed relief, surprise, and the fact that he felt impressed. He had wanted to help, but served under a martinet colonel who insisted on punctuality from patrols sent out. In the face of that letter, his colonel could raise no objections if he failed to return on the appointed day.

"We'll ride with you, sir," he stated.

"And I'll accompany you to Fort Baker to explain to your commanding officer why you left your ordered patrol," promised Lord Henry.

"Make ready for leaving, mister. I want to ride out in thirty minutes."

In the time allocated by Lord Henry, everything was prepared. A corporal and three men remained with the wagons, but all the rest of the party went along. Only Sassfitz Kane did not ride on the rescue attempt, he not having returned from skinning the cougar.

At the place where the girls had been taken, Kerry left his horse and examined the ground. He found that the scout gave an accurate picture of what happened, but learned nothing to tie the girls' abductors with the party who visited their camp a week before.

Even with so large a party, trailing them over springy turf did not come easily. The scout led the way, taking them for almost a mile before showing where more men joined the bunch they followed and then rode on to an area of shale. That surface would not hold tracks and it covered a large piece of ground with no way of the following party knowing which way the pursued went once on it.

"We could scatter and search for sign of them leaving," Dalby suggested.

"It'd be dark before we could cover half of this lot," Lord Henry replied. "If there was only some way we could follow them over the rocks."

"There's one way we might," Kerry put in, dropping from his horse. "It's a long shot, but better than nothing. Shaun!"

Obediently the big dog followed its master. Moving ahead of the party, but before stepping on to the shale, Kerry took the dog by the scruff of its neck and forced its head down toward the tracks.

"What's he doing?" asked Dalby.

"Wait and see if it works," the peer answered. "Pray God it does."

"Lay to it, boy!" Kerry ordered, as Shaun sniffed the ground.

While catching the scent picture, Shaun could not at first arouse any interest in it. Deer, cougar, bear, buffalo, he had tracked them all and understood the attraction, but never that mingled picture of men and horses. However, willingness to work had always been one of the wolfhound's good points and he moved forward slowly. Among the other scents, he caught wind of one familiar to him. By luck, Calamity had ridden Beryl's paint that morning while the blonde took Kerry's mare. On more than one occasion Shaun walked alongside the paint and knew its odor. Mingled with the odor came that of Beryl and Calamity—and mixed among it fear. All Shaun's protective instincts came to the fore. Moving forward, nose to the ground, he followed the scent-picture on to the shale.

"Can he do it?" breathed Dalby, watching the dog hesitate.

"He's hunted down animals before," Kerry replied. "Maybe he can follow them."

"Is there anything we can do?" Lord Henry inquired.

"Not a thing. He'll have to work his way across the shale, there's nothing we can do to help him except keep out of his way."

Chapter 14

A PAIR OF DESPERATE WOMEN

~~~

SEATED AHEAD OF BERYL, HER WRISTS SECURED BY cords and feet lashed to the stirrup irons, Calamity knew that she was in the tightest spot of her life. Behind her, Beryl moved in an effort to find a more comfortable way of sitting, her arms around Calamity's waist and wrists fastened.

From the moment Calamity saw the men, as she and Beryl stood looking at the elk dropped by the girl, she guessed what they were. The presence of Kerry's ex-skinner, Potter, did nothing to lessen Calamity's concern at falling into their hands. However, covered by two rifles, the girls could not escape.

Give Beryl her due, she acted in a mighty cool manner and did not lose her head. Even Calamity failed to guess what the blonde intended to do as she went to the horse. Seeing Beryl knot the reins around the saddlehorn gave Calamity a hint and when the blonde started the horse running, she pitched in with flying fists and feet. By the time the men managed to subdue the girls, it took all six of them, there was no chance of their capturing the fast-fleeing mare.

Like Calamity, Potter knew the chances of the mare finding Killem and the wagons was slight, but he preferred not to take the chance. So, although he and his companions cursed and threatened the girls, they did no more. Later they might try to put the threats into practice.

After butchering the elk and loading it on their spare horses, the men fastened both girls on Calamity's mount and pulled out. They had been gone less than half an hour when the soldiers arrived, although none of them knew that.

Just before reaching an area of shale over which Calamity knew no man could follow tracks, the men met up with another party. Any hopes Calamity raised at the first sight of the newcomers soon ended. If anything, they added to the seriousness of the situation. From what she heard, Calamity gathered that the second party had met up with a wagon load of whisky headed for some fort's sutler. Bottles clinked on every saddle and four horses each carried a load of kegs. The attitude and manner of the second party told Calamity that some sampling of the loot had been done.

What with one thing and another, the combined parties did not make good time after winding a difficult track route across the shale. Night came and the men showed no sign of stopping. Although passing the bottle freely among them, the men made no attempt to molest the girls, but Calamity knew it to be only a matter of time before something broke.

Around midnight they rode along the bottom of a wide, sheer-ended gorge. A fast-flowing stream ran to their right, tumbling in a noisy waterfall from the lip of the gorge. Once by the waterfall, the gorge swung in a gentle curve and widened out. After a quarter of a mile or so ahead, lights glinted and from the way the party's horses perked up, Calamity guessed that they approached the end of the journey.

Halfway to the lights, a voice called a challenge and received an answer from a surly, sleepy-sounding Potter. If the gang maintained that lookout permanently, sneaking up on them would be practically impossible. Not, Calamity mused, that there was any chance of her friends arriving to sneak up in the near future. Lord Henry and the others would be unlikely to start worrying about the girls' non-arrival until night fell, and by that time could not hope to find them. It would be morning at the earliest before the start of a search could be made, then the men must locate the place of the abduction and start following tracks.

"Is there nothing we can do, Calamity?" Beryl whispered, her voice calm, if tired, and mouth close to the other's ear.

"Not a blasted thing, gal," Calamity answered. "We'll just have to sit back and watch our chances."

"What're you pair yapping about?" demanded Potter, his voice slurred with sleep and drink.

"Just wondering which of Kerry, Lord Hank or Dobe Killem is going to tear out your guts when they come here," Calamity replied.

"They have to find us first, gal," the ex-skinner sneered. "Which same by morning that springy turf'll growed back up and there won't be no sign. And even if they get up here, there's three look-outs watching—and this's the only way in here."

Which ought to make the gang safe from the girls' friends. Already Potter's party had more men than Lord Henry could muster, and it seemed that the half-circle of cabins held more of them. Without the element of surprise to back them, Lord

Henry and the others could accomplish nothing. The presence of the look-outs made surprise unlikely, if not impossible.

Straining her eyes, Calamity tried to pierce the darkness and learn more about the gang's hideout. She could see little for the gorge ended in a wall beyond the cabins and its shadow hit the details she wished to learn. From what she saw, the cabins had been built to mutually support each other in the event of an attack. Most likely beaver-hunting mountain men first erected them, not that Calamity cared at the moment. There appeared to be little sign of life around the place, but some laughter and talk came from the center building. Knowing something of defense against Indian attack, Calamity concluded that the horses would be corralled behind the houses in a position where the men using the camp could prevent them being run off. Nothing she saw filled her with any great hope of rescue, or escape.

Light flooded from the door of the center cabin, illuminating the new arrivals. Several men emerged from the building, including two at least the girls recognized.

"Hey now," said Jenkins, his scarred face twisting into a leer. "What've we got here?"

"Back off, Jenkins!" snarled Potter, as the other advanced toward the girls. "They're mine."

"Yours?" Jenkins spat back. "You know our rules here. Nobody owns a thing. It's share and share alike."

"I caught her!" Potter objected, guessing that Jenkins had designs on Beryl rather than the slightly less attractive but far more dangerous Calamity.

"We all took a hand in it," one of the party pointed out.

"Hold it, all of you!" Varley said from the door of the building. "We'll follow our usual procedure and draw lots for her." He could see the idea did not meet with general approval and sought for something to divert attention. "What've you brought in, Mr. Weiss?"

"Whisky," replied the leader of the second party. "We jumped this feller with a wagon loaded with it. Figured he might be going to sell it to the Injuns——"

"No excuses are necessary here," Varley interrupted. "Our precepts are that all goods are the property of the community as a whole, not of the individual, and we are within our rights to take what we want."

"Yeah," Weiss grinned. He was a big, bulky hard-case. "Figuring that way, I reckon I'll just take me that blonde gal——"

"The hell you do!" Potter barked. "I caught her and she's mine."

"I'm boss here!" Jenkins burst in.

"*Boss?*" queried Weiss, lips drawn back in a challenging snarl. "Way your pard tells it, we're all equal and there's no bosses."

Just as Calamity hoped for the start of a fight which might give them an opportunity to escape, Varley stepped in. While lacking strength or physical courage, he possessed one thing the others lacked: the ability to use his brains.

From the start he found that his community did not come up to expectations in the matter of noble self-sacrifice necessary to make his ideals work. While all showed willingness to share other people's property, they tended to cling to their own. Since leaving the railroad, finding the cabins and gathering in a prime assortment of riff-raff and cut-throats, he had been forced to learn how to handle the lowest, most vicious and selfish type of men. There was only one way to do it, play them off against each other.

"There's no need to argue among ourselves," he told them, and they had sufficient regard for his brains to listen. "We'll put them in with the other women and settle the matter amicably."

"Not until we're all here!" put in a man wearing

a filthy U.S. Cavalry uniform. "Some of my pards aren't in yet."

His protest came less out of loyalty to his friends than from a fear of being cut out of the proceedings. While sharing the cabins and other property for mutual self-preservation, the men tended to be members of separate groups with but one thing in common, distrust of the others and determination to get their fair—meaning slightly more than the others if possible—share of whatever came into the camp.

"Naturally none of us want to make other members miss sharing," Varley replied—which might be true in his case. "I propose that we leave things as they are until morning, gentlemen."

Probably none of the others would have agreed, if he, or his group, could have been sure of forcing their will upon the rest and each section realized that any attempt on their part to force the issue would unite the remainder in opposition.

"All right," Jenkins said suddenly.

"I'll go with that," Potter continued, and the remainder rumbled agreement.

"Then it's decided. We toss them into the hut with the other women and leave them until after a democratic decision on who uses them first," Varley announced. "Shall I hold the key to the cabin?"

"We'll leave it on the hook like always," Weiss answered, and that too met with general approval.

Although Calamity felt like making a fight, she knew the futility of it. So she allowed herself to be freed and dropped off the horse. Beryl also jumped down, moving stiffly but landing on her feet despite, like Calamity, still having her wrists fastened—she had been ordered to lift her hands over the other girl's head while Calamity's feet were freed from the stirrups.

Still without making trouble, Calamity and Beryl allowed themselves to be taken to a cabin at the end of the line. A lantern hung on one hook, a key to the large padlock which secured the door on another, and a coiled bull whip upon the third. Seeing the last, Calamity wished that her hands were free. If they had been and she could once lay hands on the whip, she reckoned she could make some of them wish they had never been born.

No such opportunity presented itself. Varley unlocked the door and Weiss threw it open.

"Get in!" Varley ordered.

"Are you leaving us tied like this?" Calamity asked.

"They can't get out," Jenkins sneered. "It's been tried. Turn 'em loose."

Calamity bit down a gasp as the blood started to circulate freely on the removal of her bonds. Before she could make a move, even if she intended to, Weiss thrust her into the cabin and a moment later Beryl joined her. The door slammed and the girls turned to look around them. What they saw handed them maybe the worst shock of the abduction.

Some eight or so women slumped around in a bare, unfurnished room in attitudes of complete dejection. Dull, lifeless eyes in faces which showed almost inhuman suffering studied the girls without hope or interest.

"My God!" Beryl gasped. "What's happened to them?"

After answering the question in pungent, blistering words, Calamity went on, "They'll have to kill me first. Let's see if we can get out of here."

One look told them both that escape would be almost impossible. Underfoot the cabin's floor might be earth, but it had been packed so hard that only a pick might make an impression upon it; and even then it would be a slow process. Every window had been boarded over and securely nailed, while the walls were built of stout timber and made to last.

"We'll never break out," Beryl said, just a hint of fear in her voice. The sight of the women unnerved her more than she could say.

"And we can't stop them getting in either," Calamity replied. "I ought to have made a move out there, but I figured doing it might rile them up."

"It would have united them against us," Beryl agreed. "At least we're fairly safe while they can't agree who—who——"

"Yeah," Calamity said when the blonde could not continue. "How long have you gals been here?"

While her main aim had been to distract Beryl from thoughts of her fate, Calamity also hoped to gain information. Her words met with only dull-eyed stares at first, then at last one of the women answered.

"They—took me and my daughter, shot my husband, maybe two months back."

Slowly Calamity drew out the other women's stories and the picture painted did not fill her with hope. On their arrival more than one woman had revolted and wished she had not, or had been killed in the attempt. Try as Calamity might, she could not put spirit into the women. Not even Beryl's eloquence drove through the apathy bad food and worse treatment caused to engulf the victims of Varley's community.

"Looks like we're on our own," Calamity said after a time. She went to one of the windows and peered through a crack. "At least those yahoos aren't roaming about. Likely they're all set in that big place and watching each other."

Time dragged by with no sign of any of the men

coming. Calamity and Beryl stood by the window and, until tiredness wore them down, took turns to keep watch through the cracks. At last Calamity insisted that they tried to get some sleep. It would be of no use trying to face the men while half-dead with fatigue. If the two girls hoped to escape, they must be more alert than their captors.

While Beryl doubted if she could sleep, she found that her eyes refused to stay open. Calamity doused the light, ignoring a few feeble protests from the older prisoners. Then she and Beryl settled down on the hard floor. With Calamity's arm protectively around her, Beryl found herself nodding off to sleep.

"Wake up, Beryl gal!"

Feeling a hand shaking her, Beryl stirred and opened her eyes. At first she could not remember how she came to be in a cabin after so many nights sleeping in Calamity's wagon. Then remembrance came and she sat up, groaning a little. Chinks of light showed through the boarded-up windows, telling Beryl that day had come. She looked to where Calamity had returned to the front window once more.

"Are they coming?" Beryl asked, rising.

"Not ye——" began Calamity, then peered again through the crack. "There's one of 'em coming out of the biggest cabin. From the way he's acting, none of the others know what he's doing. This might be our chance, gal."

Beryl joined Calamity at the window and peeked through another crack. Noticing Jenkins' surreptitious glances at the big cabin, she concluded Calamity was right in the assumption that he did not want to be observed.

"He's wearing his gun," she pointed out. "Can we do anything?"

"We're going to try," Calamity replied. "This's what I want you to do."

Throwing a final cautious glance at the other cabins, Jenkins took down the key and used it to unfasten the padlock. He pushed open the door and looked into the dark interior. What he wanted stood straight ahead of him. Stepping forward, he entered the cabin, ignoring everything but Beryl. His arms reached out, took her by the shoulders and drew her his way, lowering his face toward hers.

Although scared, Beryl did not panic. She remembered Calamity's instructions and carried them out. Before the man's lips touched her, Beryl lashed up with her knee, sending it with all the force she could muster straight between his legs. Unmentionable agony ripped into him as the knee smashed home. Coming so unexpectedly, the blow paralyzed him and struck him dumb. The hands left Beryl's shoulders and she staggered back, slightly aghast at what she had done.

After standing behind it while Jenkins entered and watched Beryl, Calamity thrust the door shut with her foot and sprang forward to carry out her part. Gripped between her hands, she held her waist belt. It was the only weapon the two girls could improvise, but Calamity figured it might do the trick. As Jenkins' head jerked back in agony, Calamity threw the loop of the belt over it and drew the strong leather tight about his throat.

Instinct caused Calamity to do the right thing automatically. On drawing tight the belt, she thrust her knee into the man's back to give added leverage. If he had been uninjured, Jenkins would have found trouble in escaping. After taking Beryl's attack, he could do nothing. Not until the belt cut off his wind to a dangerous extent did he try to escape; and then his efforts were without guidance, being blind struggles which did more harm than good.

"Stop it, Calam!" Beryl gasped, staring at the man as he sank to his knees with face working in its efforts to breathe, lips swollen and tongue bursting out through them. "You'll kill him!"

The words meant nothing to Calamity for a moment, then she realized that her victim hung limp, his struggles ended. Opening her hands, she let him free and he crashed to the floor in a limp heap.

"Get his gun!" she ordered, dragging free her belt and swinging it about her waist.

Kneeling alongside the man, Beryl tried to roll him over. "He's nearly dead, Calam!" she gasped, making no attempt to take the revolver from his holster.

"And serves him damned well right," Calamity replied. "Get his gun and don't go woman on me, gal. We've got to get the hell out of here."

Realizing the fate that awaited her should she not escape forced Beryl into action. She forgot her concern for Jenkins' condition and drew his revolver. After checking that the gun was loaded, she offered it to Calamity.

"Here."

"You keep it," Calamity answered. "There's something by the door I can use a damned sight better than that."

Turning, Calamity inched open the door and peered out. There did not appear to be any sign of life so she reached out and lifted the whip from its hook. With it in her hand, she felt more secure. At least she could make a fight of it should the men come after her.

Swiftly Calamity studied the surrounding area.

She looked back along the gorge, but the angle at which the cabin had been built prevented her from seeing the trail or look-outs. Through a gap between two other buildings she saw a corral containing several horses. More important, saddles hung on the corral rail. If she and Beryl could reach the corrals, they had a chance of freeing all the horses and using two to make their escape. Beyond the corral the end wall of the gorge rose fairly steep. From what she could see, a track ran up it to a cave. If all else failed, they might climb the track and hole up in the cave. Maybe they could find something to make a fire, using its smoke in an attempt to guide Kerry's party to them. First off, though, they had to reach the corral.

"We'll split up," Calamity said. "You go along the side here and round the back. I'll make a run to that wagon there, then between the cabins and meet you by the corral."

"Why not go together?" asked Beryl.

"It'll give us two chances instead of one to make it," replied Calamity. "Maybe there'll be a gun in the wagon. It came in late this morning, maybe an hour after you went to sleep, and I don't reckon they'll've unloaded it yet. I'll take a look and see. Get going, gal."

"But——"

"No buts. Move. If you get to the corral before

I do, catch a horse and scatter the rest. Run them through this way and I'll see if I can grab one. Then we'll run down the gorge and chance the look-outs not being able to hit us as we go by."

"All right," Beryl answered. "But what if they see you?"

"Don't come back, no matter what you hear. You'll do more good by turning loose the horses. Now move."

Without wasting any more time, Beryl darted along the edge of the building and slipped between it and the next. She peered around the back corner, then began to run in the direction of the corral. A shout from beyond the cabins drew her eyes that way and she heard Calamity shriek defiance, followed by the explosive pop of the whip and the howl of a man in pain. Hesitating, Beryl looked in the direction of the sound and she tried to decide what to do. She knew what Calamity had said, but wondered if she ought to go to the red-head's aid.

Just an instant too late Beryl heard the sound behind her. She started to turn and saw Weiss closing stealthily on her. Even as she tried to raise the gun, he sprang forward. A big hand slapped the revolver from her fingers and another grasped her shoulder. A scream left Beryl's lips, brought on by the pain of the fingers crushing her flesh and fear of what would come next.

Calamity almost reached the wagon when she heard a shout and saw Potter at the door of the main cabin. Lurching forward, the man rushed at her. From the angle at which he stood, Potter failed to see the whip Calamity held. He learned of its presence soon enough.

While heavier and not so well kept, the whip did not differ so much from her own that she could not handle it. Out curled its lash, exploding in the center of the man's face and bringing a scream in answer to her shrieked-out curse. The damage had been done. Voices shouted questions in the main cabin and feet thudded as men, woken from a drunken sleep, made for the door to investigate the disturbance. Calamity ignored Potter as he staggered around in a circle with hands clutching at his bloody, agonized face. Darting to the wagon, she swung quickly up on to its box. Already the first man was out of the cabin, rushing by Potter and apparently unaware of his danger. Again the whip slashed and the man reeled away.

A noise behind her brought Calamity whirling around. She found that one of the gang had emerged from a cabin on the other side of the half-circle and was on the point of swinging aboard. Jumping forward, she kicked the man full under the jaw and sent him reeling backward to crash to the ground. A swift pivot and her whip cracked viciously before the nearest of the men from the main cabin. On its porch a man halted. He had already felt the pain of a whip's lash and knew better than to get too close. Jerking out his revolver, he lined it on the girl.

Although Calamity saw the raised gun, it was far beyond the distance at which she could do anything with the whip.

Chapter 15

A TRICK OF THE SKIN HUNTER'S TRADE

～～

"Is HE STILL ON THE LINE, KERRY?" ASKED LORD Henry, riding his leg-weary horse at the hunter's side and watching Shaun lope along, nose to the ground, ahead of them.

"I reckon so," Kerry answered. "This damned springy turf doesn't hold tracks and I've nothing to go on."

All through the night they had ridden, following the dog as he tracked the girls' abductors. Ahead a fast-running stream glinted in the morning sun and the wolfhound paused to quench his thirst before returning to the trail again. Soon after drinking, Shaun approached where the stream ran through a wide, winding gorge. The springy turf, which held a scent-picture far better than it showed tracks, began to thin down, being replaced by rocky ground. A wind blew through the gorge and tended to wipe away the scent, but it also carried the smell of men and horses with it. Shaun halted, his head rising to sniff the breeze.

"Hold it!" Kerry hissed and raised his hand. "Come here, Shaun."

Obediently the big dog returned and the men halted, awaiting orders.

"I'd say they're not far ahead," Lord Henry commented.

"He's caught a wind-scent, that's for sure," Kerry admitted. "Reckon you and me'd best move in on foot and scout the gorge."

"Certainly," agreed Lord Henry, drawing his Winchester and dismounting. "Hold the men here, Mr. Dalby."

With Shaun between them, Lord Henry and Kerry moved cautiously into the gorge's mouth. Although Calamity could not see it in the darkness, only the wall between the stream rose sheer. At the other side a fairly steep incline dotted with rocks offered a way by which men might advance unseen instead of using the trail. Gliding from cover to cover, employing the skill perfected pronghorn-hunting on the Great Plains, the two men advanced. Just after they passed the level of the waterfall and approached the curve, Kerry gave a signal which caused Lord Henry to flatten down. Wriggling to the hunter's side, Lord Henry scanned the land ahead of them.

"The girls must be in those cabins," he breathed.

"Looks that way," Kerry agreed. "See the guards?"

"There's two of them by that shelter."

"And another one a bit ahead of them. He's sat between those two rocks by the one that looks like a bear."

"I've got him," Lord Henry said, studying the nearest man, noting how he sat in a position to watch the trail and nursed a rifle on his knees. "They're alert."

Even the riff-raff Varley gathered knew the dangers of not keeping an alert watch when on guard. The nature of the hideout led the look-outs to be extra careful for they had no wish to be taken by surprise in a dead-end gorge.

"I can drop them all from here," Kerry stated.

"And at the first shot, the other two would be under cover, giving the alarm," the peer pointed out. "Getting Dobe here and the three of us shooting together won't be much better, the noise would reach the cabins."

That figured. One shot would echo loud in the

gorge; three ought to make enough of a racket to waken the men in the cabins, even happen they were asleep at that hour. From the general lack of life around the cabins, Kerry guessed that the men might still be asleep. He did not care to think at a possible caused for the camp's lack of wakefulness. Desperately he looked around him for some way in which he could reach the look-outs. Sneaking up on them would be impossible. If he could only find a way to use the rifle without it being heard——

"There's a ledge running along that wall there!" he whispered and started to move backward.

"Yes," agreed Lord Henry.

"Happen it goes under the waterfall, it'd take a man to the corner there."

"So it——" began the peer, and then realized what Kerry meant. "You've hit it, old son. Who'll do it, you or I?"

"Me," Kerry stated. "You can handle the men better than I can."

"Very well. Let's think out how to act, then make a start."

It seemed that fate had decided to side with the searching party, Kerry thought, as he moved slowly along the ledge. His rifle and bullet box, wrapped in a soldier's poncho, hung over his back and he was wet to the waist from wading the stream. Once over, he found little difficulty at first in using the ledge. Some fault in the rock, a softer layer than the rest probably, had caused a sizeable overhang and left a wide ledge that passed behind the waterfall. Spray from the fall had left a slick, green slime on the ledge behind the water, but Kerry's moccasins possessed gripping powers almost equal to the suction pads on a fly's feet. By exercising considerable care, he crossed behind the thundering water and emerged, soaked to the skin, at the other side.

Flat on his belly, Kerry crawled forward until he reached the curve and could peer around it. The situation was much like when he set up a stand to hunt a herd of buffalo. With solid rock under him, Kerry could not use his rest, but had shot prone before that day and knew his skill would be no less from such a position.

Opening the bullet box, he set it in the correct position and then fed a round into the Sharps' breech. The thunder of the waterfall almost deafened him, but he ignored the sound and lined his rifle on the nearest look-out. There was no time for moralizing, even had Kerry felt the inclination to do so. Neither girl went willingly to their abductors and might have suffered much at the hands of the men in the cabins. If Kerry's party hoped to effect a rescue, he had to prevent those look-outs giving a warning.

From his position he could see all three men clearly, but only four of the cabins and a stationary, teamless wagon remained in view. Kerry estimated ranges and gauged the wind strength so as to know its effect on his bullets. Taking aim at the nearest of the trio, he allowed for the wind and squeezed the trigger. The noise of the falling water drowned out the shot even to Kerry, and he doubted if any of the look-outs heard it. Smoke momentarily hid Kerry's first target and when it wafted away the hunter thought for a moment that his bullet missed. The man still sat between the two rocks, but his position had changed. Now the rifle tilted off one knee, its barrel gouging into the ground, while he leaned in an unnatural manner and a red trickle of blood ran down his face.

Clearly the waterfall achieved its purpose, for neither man showed any sign of concern, or even knowing that their advance scout had been killed. Reloading swiftly, Kerry altered his aim and tried to decide which of the pair he should take first. Accurate though the Sharps undoubtedly was, its single-shot capacity did not allow a rapid second bullet. While the Winchester carbine could have cut down both men before the second had time to realize what happened to the first, it lacked long-range accuracy, so Kerry had not brought it along.

One of the men rose and Kerry sighted on him,

thinking he might have noticed something wrong with the dead man and be meaning to take a closer look. Instead, he turned and peered back toward the cabins.

That settled the problem. Once again Kerry changed aim and squeezed off his shot at the man who faced him. Before the smoke cleared, Kerry was throwing open the Sharps breech and ejecting the empty case, his right hand blurred from the lever to the box. Often when a buffalo herd showed restlessness, he had used his speed to take down another couple before they broke. The speed gained under hunting conditions served him well. Slipping another bullet home, he closed the breech and never took his eyes from the two men.

Apparently the third man heard the sound of Kerry's bullet driving home, or his companion made some sound, for he turned and stood looking down. The full impact of what had happened did not strike the man immediately. Having heard no shot, he failed to grasp what the hole in his companion's chest meant for a good three seconds—by which time Kerry had reloaded and changed his aim. Even as realization came to the man and he straightened up, wildly searching for whoever shot his companion, Kerry fired again. Caught in the head by the heavy bullet, the third look-out spun around, crashed into a rock and slid to the ground.

A movement caught the corner of Kerry's eye. Turning his head, he saw Shaun loping fast along the trail. He had left the dog with the main body and could not understand what sent Shaun rushing off in such a manner. There was no time to worry about that. While he had silenced the three look-outs, his work had not ended. Lord Henry and half the men advanced on foot, darting from cover to cover in an attempt to close on the cabins without being detected. Doing so with living look-outs would have been impossible. Even without them, it was far from a sinecure. To give the others a chance, Kerry had to watch the cabins and shoot down anybody who came out and gave a sign of spotting the advancing attackers.

While altering the setting of the Sharps's rear sight, Kerry saw a figure dash from one of the hidden cabins and make for the wagon. Before he could line his rifle, he recognized the shape as Calamity Jane. Then men appeared at the various cabin doors, but their attention was on the girl and none gave a sign of noticing the approaching attackers. Kerry saw the man before the main cabin draw a gun and knew he must cut in. Taking careful aim at the man's body, as offering the easiest target, he squeezed the trigger and the rifle roared.

Even at longer ranges than five hundred yards, a Sharps rifle packed enough power to fell a bull buffalo. Its effect upon a man was even more terrible. Before he could shoot at Calamity, the man caught a bullet full in the chest. It flung him bodily backward, through the open door and into the cabin from which he had just emerged.

The body landed almost at Varley's feet as he rushed across the room to investigate the cause of the disturbance. While not being an expert in such matters, Varley needed only one glance to tell him no revolver caused that wound, or packed the power to throw a grown man backward in such a manner.

From outside came a distant but ringing bellow of "Charge!" the crackle of shots, shouts from closer at hand and a scream. Varley felt as if a cold hand touched him, realizing what the sounds meant when taken together. Turning, Varley darted across the room to the rear door. Maybe nothing would come of the attack, but he felt no harm could come from his taking precautions. He could collect a horse from the corral and lead it up the steep path of the rear wall to the cave and have all prepared for making good his escape should that become necessary.

While trying to free herself from Weiss' hands, Beryl heard the rapid patter of approaching feet and a roaring snarl. Led to her by her scent carried by the wind along the gorge, Shaun came rushing to Beryl's rescue. Weiss saw the big dog and released the girl, thrusting her aside with one hand and reaching for his gun with the other. Even as the gun cleared leather, Shaun hit the man, teeth clamping him on the arm. Pain knifed through Weiss, his arm went numb and he dropped the gun. Then Shaun's weight brought the man crashing to the ground. Like a flash Shaun changed his hold, mouth releasing the arm and driving for the throat.

Beryl felt horror-struck for an instant as she watched the dog's powerful jaws clamp on the man's throat. Then concern for Weiss ended as she realized that her own danger was far from past. If any of the men from the cabins could lay hands on her, they had a hostage to be used against her friends. More than that, she must try to carry out the duty Calamity gave her.

Bending down, Beryl scooped up her revolver in one hand and grabbed Weiss' dropped weapon with the other. She saw Varley appear at the door of the main cabin just as she reached the corral. The man started toward her, saw her raise the revolver and hesitated. Then his nerve gave way and he decided not to chance rushing the determined-looking girl. Swinging around, he darted off at an angle, heading for the rear wall of the gorge. Beryl watched the man go, then, before she could decide, found something to distract her attention.

With the look-outs down, Lord Henry led half the party on foot down the gorge. They were within fifty yards of the cabins, Calamity holding the attention of the men from the cabins, before anybody noticed them. Giving a bellow of "Charge!" Lord Henry threw up his Winchester and fired. On the heels of his shot, every man of his party cut loose in a creditable volley. Almost every member of the hunting party carried a repeating rifle and continued to shoot fast while the soldiers reloaded their Springfield carbines.

Caught under the withering blast of fire, still feeling the effects of an extensive carouse the previous night, Varley's men could not take advantage of their superior numbers. Five men went down, three more caught lesser injuries, and the rest lacked any cohesive reasoning to help them fight back. Some threw down their guns, others tried to make a fight in the open, and a few dashed for the cabins. While most of the latter found themselves singled out for attention, half a dozen, including Rixon, reached the safety of the main cabin.

Calamity saw the man with the revolver drop, but could not think how he came to die. On hearing her friends' arrival, she wasted no time in idle thought. Turning, she dived into the wagon and flattened herself down among its load. With the whip in her hand still, she figured she could dissuade any attempt to fetch her out to be used as a hostage.

Snarling in rage, Potter headed for the wagon. He aimed to either grab Calamity as a hostage, or kill her. Before he reached the wagon, a rifle bullet cut him down.

Hearing the sounds of the gun battle raging beyond the cabins, Beryl flattened down behind a rock by the corral. A call brought Shaun to her and the big dog, wise in such matters, flattened down by her side. At the main cabin, the rear door drew open again and Rixon emerged. Gripping the revolver in both hands, having laid Weiss' weapon on the ground, Beryl sighted and fired. At that range she could not hope to make a hit, nor wanted to, but her bullet came close enough to make the man change his mind.

The final break came when Lieutenant Dalby and Kerry brought the remainder of the men, each leading one of the foot party's horses, down in a charge. Seeing the newcomers, already thoroughly demoralized, the men before the cabins threw aside their guns and surrendered. Which left those fortunate enough to be under cover as a possible menace to the rescuers.

"Where's Beryl?" Kerry bellowed, sliding his gray to a halt and glaring around him.

Calamity appeared at the end of the wagon and

jumped out. "She's behind the cabins, down by the corral likely."

Ignoring the surrendering men or possible danger from those inside the buildings, Kerry charged forward. Five men followed on his heels, but Lord Henry kept the rest in hand and began securing their prisoners, or making for the cabins to see if more of the gang remained unlocated.

In the main cabin, Rixon looked at the others. None knew what to do for the best, but all wished to escape. Having no idea who handled the revolver behind the corral, they saw their escape cut off and might have thought of fighting had Rixon not been looking from one of the rear windows.

"It's Varley," he snarled. "The bastard's run out on us."

"Where's he at?" demanded another, a man who had been in the camp for some time. Crossing to the window, he looked out. "He's headed for the cave. I'm getting out of here."

Although Rixon could not see any cause for the man's sudden decision, most of the others with him knew it and wasted no time following the lead in rushing to the front door.

"Don't shoot!" yelped one of the men, throwing his gun out.

"You've got to stop Varley!" a second went on, leaving the cabin with hands in the air.

Seeing Beryl, Kerry flung himself from his horse and dashed to her. He scooped the girl into his arms and kissed her. Then moving her back to arms' length, he looked down at her.

"Did they——" he began.

"No. Oh, Kerry, I was so afraid."

"Easy, honey. It's all over now."

Twisting around, Kerry saw Weiss' body sprawled on the ground. Never had he felt more grateful to the big wolfhound than at that moment. However, before he could say anything, Lord Henry appeared with two of the gang following on his heels.

"We have to stop that blighter reaching the cave, Kerry," the peer declared.

"Why?"

"Apparently there's enough explosives in it to bring down half the gorge's walls and that's just what that blighter intends to do."

"He's damned near a quarter of a mile off," Kerry pointed out. "We'd never reach him in time, nor could Shaun even if we could lay him on a trail."

"It's Varley," Lord Henry said. "Would he do it?"

"He's vindictive enough to try," Kerry answered. "Damn it, I was in such a rush that I slid down from the ledge and left the Sharps on it."

"My Remington's on the saddle," Lord Henry said. "Quick, one of you, go and fetch it for me."

Having heard enough to realize the gravity of the situation, one of the soldiers who followed Kerry turned and dashed away. On the path, Varley climbed higher and nearer to the cave with each passing second.

"Where the hell's my hor——" Lord Henry began.

"It's here now," Kerry replied.

Springing forward, Lord Henry drew the Remington from its boot and extracted a carton of bullets from the saddle pouch. Kerry studied the climbing shape and thought fast.

"You'll need a rest," he said.

"No time to get one," Lord Henry replied.

"You'd best use my shoulder then."

Kerry crouched slightly and the peer rested the Remington's barrel on his shoulder. Carefully Lord Henry adjusted the sights, ignoring the pleas from one of the prisoners to hurry. Standing like a rock, Kerry watched and waited, hoping that the peer managed to allow for wind and all the other factors which affected accuracy at long ranges. Having seen Lord Henry shoot, the hunter knew he could rely on him to make no mistake.

On reaching the ledge before the cave, Varley paused. Fear of the consequences filled him and he knew that he could expect no mercy when the women gathered by his companions told their stories. He knew enough about Western men to believe they would never stop hunting anybody connected with the wholesale murder, looting and rape practiced by his community. Only by destroying the evidence would he have a chance of escape. Inside the cave he had the means for that escape. When realizing the kind of men his community attracted, he prepared for the day which would bring retribution. The whole wall was mined with explosives, fused and ready, sufficiently powerful to fetch down enough rock to blot out the cabins and bury any evidence which might be used against him. Nor would the explosion impede his escape. Behind the cave lay a tunnel, carved by some force of nature, which led out beyond the rim. All he need do was pass through the tunnel, light the fuse and be safe. Of course, it would be afoot, but that thought held less terror for him, a big-city man, than it would be to a dweller in the West.

For all his desire to be safe, he could not resist turning to look down. He was aware that the shooting had ended, but knew nobody from the valley could reach him in time to stop the lighting of the fuses, even assuming the attackers learned of their danger. A superior sneer came to his lips. Those poor fools, pitting their feeble wits against a man of his caliber.

He died with the sneer still there. Down below, Lord Henry took advantage of Varley's lack of movement to make sure of his aim. Never had the peer taken such care, nor put so much effort into taking sight. He knew the rifle's vagaries and took them into account. With foresight and backsight aligned, his finger tightened on the trigger. Kerry stood like a rock, even holding his breath so that no undue movement might disturb the rifle's barrel. The trigger moved back and the Remington cracked. For what seemed like a very long time—but in reality was less than a second—nothing happened. Then high up the wall Varley jerked, staggered in a circle, missed the edge of the ledge and pitched outward, to plummet down to the ground.

Chapter 16

A SATISFIED CLIENT

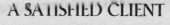

THE DEAD WERE BURIED, WOUNDED ATTENDED TO, prisoners secured. In that, Varley's community might have thought themselves fortunate. When the soldiers and members of the hunting party saw the women and heard their stories, they expressed a determined desire to apply the law of good old Judge Lynch to the survivors. Only Lord Henry's insistence on legal justice prevented what might have been a massacre. With the Englishman's sense of such things, the peer demanded that the men be taken to Dalby's fort to meet with a regular trial. The end result proved to be the same; for Varley guessed correctly about the atti-

tude of the general public to his communities'
activities.

"We'll camp here for the night," Lord Henry decided. "Then tomorrow go to the fort. I don't
think you've anything to fear, Mr. Dalby."

Nor had the young lieutenant. While his colonel
might have objected to him turning from the appointed patrol duty, circumstances made doing so
impolitic. Lord Henry saw to that.

This came later. The party spent a final night in
the camp, after Dobe Killem took a party to the
cave and defused the explosives. Next morning
they pulled out, with the army escorting the gang
and Killem driving a wagon carrying the community's prisoners.

"I hope you'll be around for the wedding,
Calam," Beryl said as she rode with her brother,
Kerry and the red-head.

"I reckon I will," Calamity agreed. "There's
nothing I like better than a wedding—as long as
it's not mine. Have you given up hunting now,
Kerry?"

"There's no reason why you shouldn't do this
sort of thing, guiding chaps like me, regularly,"
Lord Henry went on. "You've one satisfied client
already."

"And he'd have a dissatisfied wife if he tried it,"
Beryl snorted. "I'm not sitting at home while he

gallivants around hunting. There'll be too much to do getting our ranch going."

"Say, I forgot my Sharps," Kerry remarked. "It's still on the ledge. Not that I figure on needing it again. This time I'm really through hunting."

"We could leave the rifle behind then, Beryl smiled. "A kind of symbolic gesture."

"That's an idea," Kerry agreed, being enough in love to pander to his future wife's whims.

"The hell it is," said the practical Miss Calamity. "Happen you don't need it any more, take it and sell it. I never saw the gesture yet that felt as good as money. And money comes real handy when you're starting married life. That's why I never intend to save any."